☛MURDER TIMES FOUR☚

by

CHARLES NUETZEL

WRITING AS "ALEX BLAKE"

The Borgo Press
An Imprint of Wildside Press

MMVII

SECOND EDITION

☛Contents☚

☛Introduction☚

To me what is interesting about this book is that it was the first detective story I ever wrote. I was somewhat concerned and even shy about the fact, and highly pleased when the publisher/editor commented on how much he liked it! In fact, David Zentner was very complimentary about the novel.

I found the writing quite intriguing, and the novel was a mystery even to myself right up to the end. I had a couple of alternative choices for a conclusion, and just sat back and watching what the characters did. If memory serves me correctly, Mr. Zentner actually suggested the solution used in the text.

Writing can be fun at times, but most of it consists of thinking and working and thinking some more before putting the words actually down on paper. In those days of eld I was using a typewriter, of course, and any major changes or revisions to the work resulted in sometimes painful retyping of large portions of text. That made us penmen very hesitant to undertake any large-scale recasting of the manuscript. Today word processors enable authors to rewrite and re-edit almost at will. What a wonder!

So, when things ran smoothly and the thoughts flowed like the raging waters of the River Nile, it was either a great deal of fun or (occasionally) a terrible mess.

I started the book with the idea of examining the crime of rape. Does rape deserve the ultimate penalty of death? I originally didn't believe that such an assault, however brutal it might be, ought to be punished with a trip to the gas chamber. My thoughts then were young and savage and rather innocent, I have to say. Life was much cleaner and clearer to me in those days.

Now, of course, I've changed and evolved—in fact, did so to some degree even in the course of penning this novel. The book was originally called *The Rape Artist* in ms. form, and was actually published as *Love Me to Death* under the pen name, Alex Blake.

Here it is again, revised slightly and updated a bit, to be read by a new audience.

—Charles Nuetzel
Thousand Oaks, California
August 2006

☛Chapter One☚

The last thing I might have expected to hear about was murder. It wasn't the right setting; and the timing was completely off, to say nothing about the contrast between the original plan and what finally developed into a nightmare.

What I mean is, here I was with one of the most attractive women I'd ever had the pleasure of knowing; a whole weekend of fun and games to look forward to.

And the beach house was one hell of a place to be with a doll. Rustic styled. High beamed ceiling. Huge double-glass sliding doors that looked out on what the high-class writers like to call the "blue Pacific." It wasn't blue that night, though. All we could see of it were dark shadows, highlighted by bright, full moonshine. It seemed that even God-like powers of Nature were on our side, setting things up so they were romantically perfect.

A dozen groovy records lay stacked on the hi-fi player. From classy music-to-make-love-by, to some of the more progressive stuff. The lights turned down to dim; a cocktail shaker within easy reach.

Two lighted cigarettes and a lovely broad.

Well, maybe Barbara wasn't just any broad. For one thing she came on strong with a man, making him feel he was in the presence of a real-live she-cat; a hot panting nympho. She is what most people generally think of as being highly charged, in every way.

I'd met her some months before and we'd been hitting the social scene off and on, though this was the first real prolonged arrangement for a love-in. And the private beach house, owned by a buddy of mine who just happened to be out of the country at the time, helped to make things look

7

very promising.

I'm called Stanley Matson. Maybe you've read some of my newspaper pieces; I freelance a lot. To most friends, though, it is just plain ol' Stan. To Barbara Blair, Stanny-boy. Or any name she liked for all I cared, just so she called.

We'd just come in from the beach after a late evening swim, slightly tired from the sun, sand and water. And now we were relaxing before the real storm, enjoying cocktails and the nearness of one another. We hadn't even taken off our swimsuits which, considering the mood and general drift of our intentions, was something that should happen soon enough.

A slow vamp from the recorder introduced "Temptation," seductively prodding us towards the subjective matter already hammering at our minds.

"Stanny-boy," Barbara whispered, her fingers working playfully with the edge of my earlobe.

"Yeah," I managed huskily, looking down at her lovely full-bloomed breasts, hardy hidden by the brief cut of the top part of her bikini. She was on her back looking up at me with deep blue eyes, filled with dark-mystery in the dim lighting. Those perfect lips hung half open for a moment. Her face took on that expression a girl gets when she's contemplating something a lot more interesting than mere verbal conversation.

"What's that friend of yours like?" she asked.

"What friend?" It was difficult to keep my eyes off the rise and fail of her chest. Watching her breasts gently moving did things to prove that I had all my male hormones functioning overtime.

"The man that owns this place."

"Oh, interested?" I ran a finger carefully along the length of her arm. A shiver followed the progress of this caress.

"Sorta..."

"A buddy of mine. In the service together."

Her eyes met mine for an electric moment. It was like some telepathic thread attached us. I felt her fingernails dig slightly into the back of my neck. My hand gently gripped the silken, soft flesh of her naked shoulder.

8

A slight tremor moved through her.

"That buddy of yours?"

"You say one more word about him and I'll rape you right here, on the spot!" I scolded.

"That's not nice. Telling a girl you'd rape her. Shame on you."

"Well, you can drive a man beyond his limits, ya know," I grinned, deliciously excited by the way her eyes smoldered.

"I bet you're not man enough to do something like that to me," she challenged in a low, almost rasping voice.

"Well, in the first place, a gentleman wouldn't rape a woman. You're right about that."

"And what if *I* played it coy?" she mused. "You wouldn't take advantage of me? I bet you would. Bet you've had your share of virginal maidens."

"Not really. Not knowingly."

"What's wrong, do you have something against us virgins?"

"Well, put that way, not at the moment... I mean, nothing actually against, if that's what you mean."

"Well, why don't you...well, get somethin' against my virgin."

"Are you one?"

"Did you peek? Shame on you!" she giggled, then added: "Naughty boy, you! Peaking at a woman's virgin. I bet you sneak-peak down innocent girls' breasts."

"Well, when the innocent lady is wearing something as skimpy as you have on, I hardly have to peek."

"I'm not totally exposed; if you looked carefully, you'd know that." She wiggled a little, cutely causing her breasts to bounce under the tight fitting swimsuit top. "Wanna take my virginity?"

"I'd love to, but I think you already gave it away, a long time ago."

"Oh, honey, you see right through me, don't you?" She reached playfully for me. "You sure make a girl feel hot all over!"

"You sure make a man felt hot all over, too," I assured her, not moving, just gazing down at this lovely vision which was soon to be totally ravished in my arms.

"I think you're just a little wolfy boy and afraid of a real woman like me. I think you're frightened to let me see your...what do you call it? Oh, yes, you're puppy. After all, you've seen just about all of me. And I've seen nothing much of you."

"I think you're the shy one." I countered, touching her creamy white shoulder. "Scared to let a man really ravish you with his eyes."

"Only with his eyes? Oh, honey, I want the big bad wolf to come out and play with my virgin!"

"He's a respectable fella. And not so quick to expose himself to respectable women."

"Who said I was respectable?"

"Well...aren't you? You'd have fooled me any day of the year."

"Want to know the truth? I think you don't find me desirable. You aren't overwhelmed enough by the site of my lush, lovely, passion filled body to just rip my clothes off and ...have your way with me."

"What in the world makes you think that?" I cried, leaning over and touching her naked side with my hand. Slowly I caressed upwards until my fingers were covering one full, ripe breast.

"Is that the best you can do?" she scolded, pushing my hand away. "If you don't behave, I'll just leave!"

"Sure you will. I just bet!"

She burst out laughing then and grabbed my hand, crushing it into her breast, which surged up against the palm.

"Maybe it would be thrilling to be raped," she murmured in a contented voice. "Then I'd know you just couldn't control yourself."

"Who wants to control themselves?" I offered, letting my other hand run the full length of her arm until my fingers locked with hers. "At least not under these circumstances."

She squeezed my hand gently, and then said: "I wonder what it would be like to be forced. Well, forced is the wrong word. Having a man so crazed to possess me could be...rather thrilling. Know what I mean? I don't mean...well, being really forced against my will, but having a man so violently overwhelmed with desire that he wouldn't let anything stop him until he had consumed—"

"You have some wild ideas." I chuckled, looking down into her half-lidded eyes. She was so damned beautiful that I found it difficult to continue our silly little conversational word-game.

"Well," she announced, wide-eyed, "I wouldn't want to be forced against my will! But I've often wondered if it is as terrible as they make it out to be. I mean, of course it is a horrid thing to have happen. Painful and all that. But...giving men the death sentence. After all, it doesn't kill a woman! Does it?" She was suddenly thoughtfully considering that. "I suppose I should be the one saying castrate the man, hang his balls on spikes, then chop off his arms, legs and liver!"

"Geeze. You're sure are the violent one."

"I don't think so."

"And what's the liver have to do with it?"

"Live, life, death. Liv...er!" She laughed. "But seriously, and I know I'm talking with my head, not my gut, I don't think the man should be killed—put away for life, maybe but...killed?"

"What in the hell brought on *this* conversation!" I cut in, a little puzzled and annoyed. "I'm not about to violate you against your will, so why be concerned with such morbid thoughts?"

She smiled generously and then said: "It is a silly conversation, isn't it?"

"Right here and now it seems damned foolish! Because if you keep it up I *will* all but rape the hell out of you!" I moaned, suddenly feeling the strong effects of her voluptuous body so erotically revealed in the two piece suit. "Breasts like yours could make a man go insane with desire, especially under the present circumstances and— "

"There's something wrong with the rest of me?" she pouted, winking.

"Who said anything about the rest of your lush, beautifully packaged body?"

"If you keep handing out that kind of line I'll just demand that you unwrap the package—if you don't get on

11

with it pretty damn soon," she laughed, patting my cheek.

"Quite frankly all I want to do right now is to get all naked with you and discover what we've been missing out on these last few, foolish minutes!"

"Well, what's keeping you? If you don't get started soon …well at the rate you're going now it might take all night!"

"Think so?" I replied with a grin.

But I didn't move immediately. A slight breeze blew through the open, sliding glass door, bringing the scent of her delicate perfume to my already over-active sense of smell. In fact, by this time, everything about me was beginning to become quite anxious to over-act. This lovely creature of temptation did things like that to me in a big way.

The pounding in my temples was almost becoming an inner earthquake of wanton anxiety.

She smiled, parting her lips. Then her arms reached around my neck, pulled hard, drawing me toward that lovely dimpled mouth surrounded by one of the most attractive faces I'd ever seen.

Her lips trembled under mine.

Just as we merged together a thing happened straight from some corny movie or novel:

The phone rang!

At first I thought it was part of the musical arrangement coming from the record player. Maybe that's because I wanted it to be only in a recording.

This definitely wasn't the time or place to break things off.

The phone rang again!

And it *wasn't* part of any jazzy musical arrangement.

Barbara stiffened against me. Her body did things some people might not consider quite decent. I was not one of those prudes. And there was no question about the quality of the performance.

The phone rang once more.

"Forget it. "She pleaded.

I let out a groan of anger and jumped to my feet before she had a chance to get a real good hold on me.

Take care of the phone first! I figured. *Then continue*

12

with the more important physical conversation we're sharing.

"Be back in a moment," I managed to say, moving past the recorder and hitting the "off" switch. The music died abruptly, much like the angry heat of my passion had suddenly cooled down. Then, stepping to the over-working phone, I picked up the receiver.

"Yes? Matson speaking!" I grumbled in a voice heavy with irritation.

"Stanley Matson?" a man asked. He sounded like someone I'd known in the service: the first sergeant.

"Yes, Stanley Matson!"

"This is police Lieutenant Johnson. I think you should come down to the—"

"What the hell are you talking about?" I demanded, more irritated than puzzled now; and just plain mad.

"I got your number from the answering service. It's important!"

"Nothing can be *that* important!" I started to hang up the phone.

"It's about your sister!"

Lynn? What could have happened to her now? my mind wondered, as I got a better grip on the receiver. "What's she got into now?"

"It's not so pretty... "The voice lingered in space, dwindling to nothing. Then it picked up again. "If you'll come to the city morgue..."

That's all I heard. That's all I wanted to hear. I just stood there in a state of shock.

Barbara had obviously noticed my reaction because she came over and stood beside me. "What is it?"

That snapped me out of it — for the moment.

"Why?" I questioned the receiver, already knowing the only possible reason: *identification.*

My mind was spinning; I couldn't think. But my lips seemed to have a will all their own. They asked: "What happened?"

"You better come down. I don't want to talk about it over the phone."

"Damn it all, *what happened?*"

"Well...she's been killed!"

I must have been a state of shock for some minutes after that.

I don't remember getting dressed or going to the car. Luckily there was Barbara. She drove.

All I could think of was my sister Lynn.

All the troubles we had experienced in the last few years seemed painfully shallow in so many ways. Both of us lived a rather free-spirited wild life, I suppose. I was sorta drifting from writing job to job, usually doing it freelance. Punching a time-clock wasn't my idea of a real swinging life. And, annoyingly enough, Lynn had fashioned her life pretty much along the same lines her "big brother" lived. To me, that wasn't really all that respectable a way for a little sister to act. It was one thing for a guy to play the field for fun and games, but a woman should settle down, raise a family and do all those kinds of "respectable" things. I know. Terribly petty of me; and narrow minded. Especially considering that the kind of ladies who turned up in my bed weren't the marrying kind—nor was I considered a prime catch! "You're not responsible enough, to be targeted for marriage!" one wild woman told me, laughing in delight at that fact. I'd considered that a compliment, 'cause it meant this kind of woman really enjoyed my company. No strings attached. Great woman that she was! But I felt somewhat conflicted about my sister. So, when she turned out a bit wild, we simply parted company. She walked out and lived her life. I lived mine. I kept remembering how it had been when she was born—such a little creature. Having a kid sister had, at the beginning, seemed strange. A first child feels a sense of jealousy about a new baby in the family. There's the feeling that your own private world has been invaded by an alien being. You aren't quite sure if you like it! Then pride, love and a sense of protectiveness replace the feeling. I'd watched over her from childhood in a very brotherly fashion, knocking the block off of any other kid who might try to bully her; later keeping a sharp eye on the guys she dated, to make sure that they didn't take advantage of my sister. There were vacations when we shared first experiences; seeing places like the Grand Canyon, going to San Francisco and thrilling to

14

Chinatown, seeing Mexico and the bull fights. Comforting her when she was being punished for some childish prank.

Many thoughts raced through my mind, mingling together into a web that clouded over the later years.

We'd been so close that by the time we became adults, the two of us had become too much alike. The difference being that Lynn was a woman; and I just couldn't accept her ideas of morality! Well, not for a sister. For somebody like Barbara, and me that was different. But Lynn had a love for the swinging life.

The next thing I knew was that Barbara, who was driving, had stopped my car.

"We're here, Stan."

Then we walked down a long hall. After that a huge man introduced himself.

"I'm Lieutenant Johnson." He looked deadly serious, yet there was bulldog kindness in his eyes. "I'm sorry about the way I had to break this to you."

He motioned us forward.

"It isn't pretty, but you need to go through this."

"Who did it?"

"We don't know."

I felt a light-headed sickness. "What the hell are you doing to find out?"

"Easy. We're doing our best. We have men on the case, right now. I'm handling it, personally." Then he motioned us into a room. "This way. Maybe the woman should stay back. It isn't a pretty sight."

I was still dazed, emotionally. Shock does strange things to a man. You move, act, think, and yet refuse to feel too greatly. It was a condition that would stay with me for several long, anguished days.

Then we were standing over a long table. The lieutenant lifted a clean, white sheet.

I looked down at the woman's body. At first I could not accept this as belonging to my sister. The head was caked with blood where something hard had made a nice size dent.

The lieutenant was talking. "The head was fractured and probably brought on almost immediate death. She couldn't have been aware of what happened after that—"

I thanked God for this fact.

Lynn's body was cut and caked with blood. Her breasts had been slashed, the nipples sliced off. Her thighs, stomach and legs brutally opened with a knife.

"We believe she was raped first, before …the knife came into play. Probably the guy hit her first and then assaulted her body. Sexual degenerates of this kind will cut-up the woman's body after having raped her. It is all part of the rage and passion and—"

I didn't hear any more.

I just continued to look at the body and slowly, an acceptance hardened within me. This was my sister.

Lynn...my sister Lynn, baby sister Lynn! My mind screamed; sick.

The face had been badly beaten; the nose and lips were swollen. Her throat was bruised while the rape artist apparently choked out whatever life was left in her.

My mind struggled with visions of the possible scene. Someone had hit her head, choked her. Then stripping this young body naked, raped the hell out of it. Afterwards, taking a knife the beast madly slashed at the body that probably gave him a perverted sexual thrill.

It looked like she had been run through a meat grinder and somehow managed to remain more or less in one piece.

It took only one look. That was enough to make anybody sick. Never before had such a sight made me so violently ill; and in the war I'd seen plenty of terrible things; men with arms blown off and blood flowing all over the place: others with their guts hanging out, the thick gray worm-like things pulsing, red-smeared. Headless bodies dripping with crimson.

But this sight was personal. That's when it hits home really bad!

My little sister, Lynn. Young kid who got into too much trouble; nothing ever terribly serious. She'd been just too wild, maybe; but nobody deserved such a brutal end.

My mouth was filled with acid and my stomach twisted into such a tight knot that it felt like a gigantic

16

cramp. My hand, where it clawed over my tight lips, was covered with a slimy sickness.

"Oh, God. Good Lord!" I heard my voice. Then suddenly something snapped inside my head. The sickness left. A hard hatred slipped into my body, jerking it rigid. Fury pulsed like a throbbing ache, making everything around me sharp and cold. "Where's the bastard? Where's the dirty, goddamn bastard that did this?"

Every muscle tightened into hard steel. I felt myself shaking violently.

Sanity had broken; I wasn't even being rational. All I wanted to do is give my hands on the monster who had done this to Lynn.

Everybody was looking at me in surprised horror.

"Where is he? *I'll kill the bastard!* I'll rip his guts out with my bare hands!" I screamed, turning toward the lieutenant. *"Where is that bastard?"*

Johnson shook his head from side to side. "Take it easy, mister. Take it easy."

"You take it easy!" I yelled back. "Just tell me where he is!"

"We haven't got him yet. Just take it easy. We have the force doing everything possible... "

"That's not enough! Not enough by a damn mile!"

A moment later I was outside, standing on the street. The world seemed suddenly cold and deathly impersonal. Only one thought kept going round and round in my head.

Get the dirty bastard who did this, and beat the living guts out of him—slowly...ever so slowly!

Barbara was standing next to me.

"You better go home!" I told her, not even turning in her direction.

"No," she said in a soft voice. "I'll stay with you. You'd better do what the Captain said. Take it easy. What you need is a friend."

"I said go home!" I ordered, moving toward my car.

She slid in beside me and handed me the keys.

We didn't say a word until I'd stopped the car at her apartment. Then she said: "Sure you won't come up? Running around aimlessly by yourself won't help much."

"Forget it, babe!" I snapped, slamming the door behind her. "I want to be alone!"

I shifted the car into drive. "I'll call you..."

It wasn't so much that I wanted to be alone as to be free to start the search. A search for a man I didn't know. A man, who had brutally beaten up, raped and killed my kid sister.

A man I intended to find, bang around until he wished he was dead—until he begged me to kill him—and then blow the dirty bastard's brains out!

That much I promised myself; gunning the car away from the curb, leaving Barbara alone on the sidewalk outside her apartment.

☛Chapter Two☚

I don't know how long I drove. There wasn't any destination in mind. Just wandered aimlessly; thinking about the past, for the most part. A person gets to thinking about a lot of things when they are in the disturbing sort of mental condition that I was in. Mostly you worry about what you wished you'd done—not so much what you had done. No regrets about some of the blowups Lynn and I had in the past—and we had plenty of them.

We loved each other as much as a brother and sister could. Yet in many ways we hated each other's guts. Maybe because we were both so much alike. Maybe we were each looking for something different in the other.

She had always wanted a *big brother*—like a father image, I guess. That was because she'd never really known Dad. He died when we were both quite young. I remembered a little about him. He was tall and big in stature and personality. He was the type of father Lynn would have liked—and had needed. Mom died when I was in the army. That left Lynn, at the age of nineteen, to make her own way.

She'd become a little wild. And I'd wanted a sister with all the innocence that a storybook sister is supposed to have.

Lynn had her first real affair before she was eighteen; but he wasn't the first boy she'd been with. I didn't known about that until after I had returned from the army and we had gotten into one of our usual arguments. The man she was running around with wasn't the type of guy that I thought was good enough for my "little sister." He was too much like me. I saw through him; knew exactly what he was after. But I made the mistake of stating my views on the subject, and she hit the ceiling.

"What kind of woman do you think I am?" she screamed, raising on her tiptoes in order to make herself seem taller.

"That's just it. You're *not* a woman. Just a kid, wet behind the ears," I'd stormed back.

"That's all you know!"

"Oh, hell! Get off it. You don't know the first thing..."

"Don't be so sure about that!"

"You're just a kid!"

"I know the ropes!"

"Big deal! You kiss a slob. Mug around a little and think you're a real sexy bitch in heat!"

"Boy, are you living in the dark ages!" she sneered at that last remark of mine. "Don't kid yourself. Little sister Lynn has been putting out a bit to the boys for one hell of a long time!"

That was the blow that really rocked me on my heels.

"Since I was fifteen I've known the score. Probably more than you do!"

I guess I'd lost my temper then. The slap I lashed out across Lynn's face almost knocked her off balance.

I'd turned around after that and walked out of the house, heading for a bar to get loaded.

When I'd returned Lynn wasn't there.

I'd done a lot of thinking during the drinking bout. One thing I was forced to face: Lynn was over twenty-one and there wasn't really anything that I could do about her private life. If she wanted to be an easy lay for the first man who came along I couldn't do anything about it. So it hurt. But it really wasn't any of my business.

So much for innocence concerning my younger sister.

It had hurt for a long time. A huge gap shut down the bridge between us after that. We still had the love but just kept out of each other's way.

I got an apartment. Carried on with the ladies of my life. Met Barbara. Lost track of Lynn. Ran around with a lot more women. Dated Barbara. Dated some of the broads at work. Dropped interest for Barbara. Took up with Barbara again. Arranged a weekend interlude. Set things up real nice. Stocked with plenty of booze; atmosphere; and then, having set the scene, brought on the actors.

Sexy Barbara Blair. A woman who didn't know how to stop when it came to living it up; a small town girl who'd decided she might be able to make a go at show business. A kid who couldn't make it in the movies.

And what happens?

The whole deal gets blown! And I couldn't have cared less.

It was surprising to discover how superficial the sex urge can be when it comes to real important things.

We'd planned a lost weekend; and now it was really lost, all right—completely bombed out. And it didn't make any difference. In fact, the way I felt, I began to wonder just what it was that a person saw in the whole thing.

Sex. Rape.

Now the two words seemed to blend into one. Their meaning got all mixed up in my mind until I couldn't see one without seeing the other.

Barbara with her full, voluptuous breasts, large flaring hips.

Lynn, with her dainty figure. Boyish breasts. Almost narrow hips.

Barbara alive and pulsing with passion.

Lynn dead and not feeling any more the torment, after being terribly violated. Beaten to death. Strangled. *Raped!*

How could I help thinking of sex and rape as the same thing? They were so interlocked in my mind that I started seeing Barbara's body in the hands of an insane little man who was slowly tearing the clothes from her wildly writhing figure. As the last shred of clothing fell from her, her mouth opened wide, letting out a scream of sheer joy.

Barbara had become Lynn in the last mental picture.

All his efforts spent for no reason. Because Lynn would have let him have her, just for the asking.

Lynn would have given herself willingly to the little bastard.

Yet she had died. Being raped.

That was a dirty, damn shame. A rotten, dirty damn shame.

I couldn't think straight for a long time. The road seemed to blur. I heard the explosive honking of a car in front of me. Headlights blinded me. My reflexes took over, swinging the wheel to the right.

I just missed instant death.

That was enough warning. I parked the car. My mouth was suddenly dry. I needed a drink. And bad. There was the flashing red neon sign saying "C-O-C-K-T-A-I-L-S" half a block down the street.

I turned off the engine, got out of the car and started walking. It seemed I'd just begun when the entrance loomed up in front of me.

It was a cheap place. A pick-up joint. Loud and noisy. A small combo playing rock and roll in the corner. That was one kind of beat I didn't normally liked, but it perfect for this evening—sometimes a person gets in the mood for self torture and that's the way I felt tonight.

Sitting at the bar I ordered a double shot of whiskey. The singing of an over-worked drum hammered at my ears. It helped to clear away the confusion.

I had to think; but think less emotionally, more rationally.

The drink came and I quickly ordered another one before the bartender could leave. I wanted to flow right out of my head and this was the quickest way I knew.

After the second drink 1 began to think a little more rationally.

The first thing I had to face was my lack of information. I didn't have any way of knowing who this killer was; or even where to look for him.

Several other points came to mind in a quick series: I had to get to him before the police did. They were going after him with a professional and highly trained squad of men. I didn't even know where Lynn had been assaulted. Was she out on a date at the time? And was he her date or somebody else's?

Or had she been alone in a place like this—hoping to

be picked up?

I was sick inside. I didn't know the first place to start or even much about Lynn's social activities. I hadn't seen her more than once every couple of months during the last few years. I rarely talked to her on the phone. As to her activities, I had no idea what they were. One thing was clear: I had to start from scratch. Just like the police. Except they'd already had a few hours lead and that might be all they needed.

One: they knew where the crime had taken place.

I might be able to get that information from Lieutenant Johnson.

That would be the place to start. Then, go to her apartment. Find out who her friends were.

I didn't even know that.

This realization amazed me. Not until then had I given much thought to how little I actually knew about Lynn. Not even where she worked; who she ran around with; where she went; what she had....

Had?

It was hard thinking in past tense about Lynn. Even as little as we'd seen each other, we had basically been close; Even if we had been running around in different social circles.

The same *kind* of social circles; but different. Well, anyway, I *did* have one lead that the police didn't. It was slim but better than nothing. It might channel me into another direction than the one they'd take. It could be a shortcut to the killer.

I knew how Lynn thought!

I'd be able to rebuild a clearer picture from any facts, once I gathered them; because Lynn and I had always thought very much alike. Almost exactly alike.

All I'd have to do was to take the facts as they presented themselves to me and reconstruct them in the shape that seemed most logical from my viewpoint — *which was sure to be very much the same way she'd have originally lived them.*

Now, for the first time since I'd heard the terrible news, I had a plan of action. A method.

Tomorrow I'd start. Lt. Johnson, first. Then Lynn's room...

There wasn't any time to waste. I could start that very moment. Go to Lynn's apartment. See what leads I might find there. At least that would put me much closer to the fiend who had killed her. It would be a beginning—which might end... where?

That stopped me: the thought about tomorrow. There wasn't any reason for me not to start right then. The police had already begun.

Calling the barman over, I ordered a shot of whiskey with a water chaser. The moment he brought the drink I downed it. After paying the man I got up from the barstool and walked out of the place, down the street to my car. Once in the driver's seat I felt almost stone sober.

First stop: Lynn's apartment. Second stop: Anywhere! Anywhere the trail led. Just so it led to personal revenge and satisfaction.

☙Chapter Three❧

One thing I could say for Lynn's taste, it had been good. That is, in the line of apartments. She hadn't spared any expense. I'd seen the place a couple of times before but several bold changes had been made since then.

One: she had several original pieces of art on the wall. They were good. So good that I went up to see who had painted them. The signature read: Lynn M.

It was the first time I'd known she'd gone in for painting. But that wasn't saying much, since I didn't seem to know very much about her adult life.

There wasn't any difficulty getting into the apartment. The landlord quickly offered me his key after I'd proven my identity.

"I'm terribly sorry to hear about... she was such a nice young lady. Had a lot of men friends."

"Would you know any of their names?"

"No. There were too many of them. They all seemed quite nice though. Artistic types. But not *bums.*"

"Thanks. I'll just go up and.... "

"Sure. Take your time."

One fact had been gathered: she ran around with an artistic crowd. And you couldn't tell about these arty people; they're all a bit nuts anyway.

After that build-up, a person would expect a real oddball living setup. But it was quite modern In fact; her bedroom was expensive Chinese modern. My first reaction was: *too* expensive for a working girl. Then the next reaction was a question: had the apartment come furnished?

I'd find that out when I saw the landlord again.

For a long time I didn't know where to start. After

walking through the four rooms I came back to the living room and circled aimlessly about. It's amazing how confusing it can get trying to decide where to start on a search for something you don't know, for sure, even exists—or what it is, for that matter!

Several things I did notice, though.

Bookcases: Filled, for the most part, with mystery novels, science fiction and a lot of philosophy and art books. Also, a small bar in the corner of the room. Curiosity caused me to look into the liquor supply. The half-filled quart of Demerara Rum invited me to fix a drink. The thick, dark brown molasses rum flavor slowly trickled down my throat like a little rivulet of warm lava. It helped to calm the nervous fluttering of my stomach. Ever since I walked into the room it had been hard to keep the anguish from overcoming my emotions.

One thing was important: keep down the fury, the sorrow, the pain and the anger until I found the bastard that had done such a horrible thing to Lynn. Keep the emotional hate concentrated on *him*. Keep a cool! And *then, once I find him,* let it out like the exploding eruption of a volcano.

The trickle of rum thickened to a large swallow that hit my gut like a bucketful of acid. That helped a lot. Now I could think a little clearer. Maybe, more dramatically. But regardless of the actual effect, the liquor was now making it easier for me to start my search.

It was like moving through an endless sea of disconnected items. There was only one way to start. Start at the center and work outwards, until I'd examined everything in the place—from floor to ceiling.

I don't know how long it took. I just circled slowly, looking, first, at everything. From chair to table. Bookcase. Cupboards. Drawers. Just looking for anything that might tie her up with a few activities; and places; and people.

There was a matchbox. It was from *The Jungle Strip.* I knew the place. A quick pick-up, strip hangout. If a guy was low on women and didn't care what he got, then this was the place to go. I'd been there with a friend once, a couple of years before. I had never gone back.

That made one stop-off to investigate.

26

Then I started searching carefully around the room. More than just looking. Time passed. I discovered checks. The bank and branch where she kept her money. A little later, in the bottom desk drawer, I found withholding forms. She worked for an insurance company. It gave the address. That would be another place to start.

The only trouble was that I probably had discovered only the same information as the police, no doubt, already knew. I'd be one step behind them. The landlord told me that the police had been there earlier.

I went back to the bar for another drink. Then I saw something else: an ashtray that had come from the *Restaurant Bar & Grill*.

I didn't know if that would help but I had to latch onto every possible lead I could get.

The second drink suddenly made me sleepy. How many hours I'd been searching I had no way of knowing. I was completely exhausted. It must have been late.

Looking at my watch I saw it was much later than I imagined. Almost four in the morning.

The place was in a mess. Chair and sofa cushions thrown everywhere. Papers making an uneven pattern all over the floor. Books scattered. Every piece of furniture was out of place. A storm bolt had hit the place. It seemed incredible I'd done all this in such a short period of time. Even if it had been hours. I was abruptly too tired to continue any longer. What I needed, more than anything right then, was a little rest. My mind was already numb and dazed. Even vision was beginning to distort and become blurred.

I moved into the bedroom and lay down on the large, king-size bed. Sleep slammed me down like a first act curtain.

It seemed like I'd just closed my eyes when I heard the sound. It was a creeping, careful sound. Movement. A person quietly walking around.

I opened my eyes.

Somebody was moving around in the front room. Slowly, very careful not to make any sound, I slid off the bed and stepped to the half-open doorway, which led into the living room.

27

A striking silver-blonde-haired woman was bending over in my direction. Although the suit she wore didn't reveal anything beyond a few inches of neckline it was enough to charge any man's instant attention and desire to see more.

Her eyes were looking down when I first saw her. But the surprise at seeing such an attractive woman caused a gasp of amazement to shoot past my teeth.

She looked up. Jumped as if she were shot. A shocked yell sounded from her—high-pitched but intriguing in its throaty quality.

She started to move toward the front door and I leaped forward to intercept her. She was fast but luckily, not fast enough…for I got there first.

"Who, might I ask, are you?" she demanded in a tight, clipped voice of authority.

That was unexpected.

"I think that question should be reversed. Who are you?" I countered quickly.

"I don't think it's any of your business!" she shot back, standing her full height which was just under my own six feet.

I thought: the right level for a perfect kiss.

It was funny how sex could loom up suddenly and unexpectedly. But this was one high-classed package. It would have been hard for anybody to keep from admitting she had all that it took to make a man hot with desire. Raw, classy sex.

Tall. Slender. Regal. Maybe *too* regal. The high-society kind. Her hair done up in style—silver and a streak of pure gray-white running through it. She looked like something out of *Vogue,* though a wee-bit more voluptuous. The kind of lush body that makes a man want to totally explore.

Neat, pink lips. Silver fingertips. One hand was clutching white gloves. Her eyebrows were arched, almost severe looking. If it weren't for her eyes, which seemed to sparkle deep down under the make-up, she might have appeared to be as cold as ice. As cold as she was attempting to look.

We stood there, looking at each other for several silent moments. Then she backed up.

28

"Who are you?" she demanded once more, starting to cross the room, either from nerves or fear of me—I didn't know which.

"Well, under the circumstances I think it's *you* who should explain your presence. The manager knows about me, but how about you?"

I pulled out a cigarette and lighter, in a very casual act, hoping to communicate a more relaxed attitude. "Want one?"

She shook her head. By now she was considering me in a more serious fashion, calculatingly.

It was as if we were play-acting. Each of us actually working for time, trying to figure the other out. Shadow boxing like well-trained boxers.

"Well, if you must know," she sighed, in that superior voice which "blue noses" use whenever speaking to an inferior, "I have business here!"

Now, that was just about as far out of place as she could have gotten and it was impossible to keep from laughing, even though the situation was far from funny. Maybe it was nerves, letting off steam when I'd been wanting to cry like a baby.

The laughter didn't last long. She wouldn't let it. "I don't see what's so funny!"

"Well, you should," I blurted out, now beginning to feel the first edge of anger. "It so happens I'm Lynn's brother...and I don't see what..."

"Oh?" her voice had the air of contempt in it, as if she were saying: *oh, so that explains your existence...*or, *oh, you're that horrible creature I've been hearing about.*

"Lynn mentioned you—once." That was filled with her low-key contempt, too.

"Get off that crap!" This phooey air of hers was getting me where it hurt most. I could smell a fake a mile away; and I didn't feel like playing along with her little game. "Let's get down to earth. I think you might explain..."

"Mister Matson, I don't think I have to explain anything to you!" Without another word, and before I could recover from that added attack, she was on her way toward the door.

"Hey, wait!" I ordered, leaping toward her. My hand reached her shoulder just as she was about to open the door. I pulled her around so that she faced me.

We were only inches apart and her face—that close—suddenly lost all its elder superiority. It tensed in shocked fear. Through that expression and the make-up, which I could now see was well painted on; she looked a lot younger than I'd thought. The dress and image were far more mature. But in reality she was somewhere in her late twenties. Just right for picking.

But I wasn't in the mood to be looking for her more interestingly obvious charms.

"Would you mind, *please,* letting go of my arm?" she asked in a cold, forceful voice. "I don't like being handled by..."

"Look here," I interrupted, starting to release my hold on her shoulder. "Cut the attitude! I don't like it!"

"Then, in that case, I'll leave." She started to move away.

I grabbed her by the jacket.

"Just stay put!" I moved around and closed the door which she had just managed to open. "I want a few words with you. And you can cut out the crap and act like a lady – if that's not beyond your abilities!"

She looked icily at me, and then half smiled, shrugged. "I guess I was rather rude at that!"

She turned as if to walk into the room. Then she was once more facing me, but this time pointing an automatic in my direction. She must have gotten it from her handbag. But in such a skillfully rapid, flowing motion that it took my breath away. "I'm so sorry to be leaving you, Mr. Matson, but I have business elsewhere."

At five in the morning?

"I do wish you'd stay." I backed up and stepped aside as she passed. "But under the circumstances I guess I'll just have to let you go..."

That's when I lunged for the gun. My hand chopped at her wrist, numbing the fingers that held the weapon. She wasn't expecting it. Her voice yelled in a muffled scream. The automatic fell from her fingers, landing on the floor with a loud clatter. I followed it. A moment later the icy metal was clutched in my hand.

I looked up. She wasn't there. The door banged shut. I opened it. Walked into the hallway just in time to see her heading for the stairs.

I ran after her.

It's amazing how fast a woman can move when she has to. They forget to be lady-like. They move like a deer. Speed is their keyword. And this young lady was making most track stars seem like backward snails. Even so, I had almost caught her when I stumbled.

I had to reach for the railing to gain my balance. It didn't occur to me to threaten her with the gun and by then she was too far ahead to catch up.

By the time I got into the lobby she was already outside. I followed.

A car pulled away from the curb. It must have been waiting for her there. A man was driving.

Well, that was that!

Breathing hard I stood there trying to read the license number. I got the last number just in time, before it went out of focus.

A California licenses. That was a good start. From there, I'd be able to trace…. That's when it occurred to me: I might *not* be able to trace the license. If I were a cop, that would be different. But instead I was just a Joe-slob. Only in the movies or cheap novels does the hero have those kinds of connections. The chances of tracing the license number were pretty slim—to nothing! But if I ever saw the car again, I'd know it.

And that was a great help. It shouldn't take any time at all for me to find one blue car out of a million or so. Then all I had to do was to see if its license had the proper number on it. That was sure to get me nowhere!

Super private dick. *That*, I wasn't!

And even if I did find the car, I still might not find the woman. Anyway, how did I know that she really fit in with Lynn's murder? In fact, how could she?

It didn't seem to add up in the least. What did she have to do with Lynn? And what had she been looking for in

31

the first place? How had she gotten into Lynn's apartment? A key? And where'd she get the key?

Questions. Questions with no logical answers.

Nothing added up. But that didn't seem too strange. I didn't have enough of the parts of the equation to discover what X meant.

Mr. X! The man who had raped and killed my sister. The man I was after. Along a trail which had already led me to a young, high-society woman, a matchbox and an ashtray. Three leads. Plus, where Lynn worked and banked. And the automatic. Don't forget that, dummy. I put it in my pocket and walked toward my car.

It didn't occur to me that I was leaving Lynn's apartment in shambles with the door wide open. I wasn't in any state of mind to think much about any such details. I was too tired even to walk up to Lynn's place and sleep there. I wanted to go to my own place. Think things out and then look up police Lt. Johnson.

That would be the next step. Maybe he would trace the license plate number for me. Sure, he would do it, if I gave it to him, but would he tell me to whom it belonged?

Maybe I should have been more careful. But how was I supposed to have known what would happen in Lynn's apartment in the next couple of hours? Later that morning I'd find out. But that would be too late to do anything about it. Right then, all I was concerned with was getting some rest in the peace and quiet of my own old surroundings. I wasn't even thinking logically or straight. A person gets that way, sometimes; especially when they are tired. And I was dead tired.

Tired of thinking.

Tired of looking and searching.

Just plain tired; just when things were only starting up. Maybe, in the long run, it was a good thing that I got some rest, for in the next couple of days I'd need the strength that it gave me.

I was going to need it.

☛Chapter Four☚

I couldn't have slept more than a couple of hours when the doorbell rang. Foggily I struggled out of bed, trying to adjust my eyes to the light. I half staggered to a chair where my robe was lying. After tightening the band around the middle of the robe, I walked to the front door. The ringing had continued several times since I'd awakened, as if somebody was in a terrible hurry to get to me.

"Who is it?" I asked sleepily, opening the door.

"This is the police," one of the two men said as they stepped into my apartment.

"Make yourself at home, by all means!" I offered, a little irritated.

"You Stanley Matson?" the other one asked.

"Who else did you expect to find here?"

"Well, you're wanted down at headquarters for questioning."

"What the hell?"

"Come along quiet-like, and nobody gets hurt."

"Mind telling me what this is all about?" I asked, trying to gain time to shake the sleepy numbness from my brain.

"They'll tell you all about it. You better come along..."

"You don't mind if I get dressed, do you?"

"Make it quick, we don't have all day, and the Lieutenant is in a rush to..."

I didn't hear the rest. I was trying to think. Why did they want me? Questioning about Lynn? But why all the fuss? They could have just given me a call over the phone asking me to come down. This looked like an arrest and I

33

couldn't see any reason why they would want to arrest me. I hadn't done anything—*yet!* And the law can't arrest a guy for what he plans or wants to do. You have to be caught in the act or after the act. I planned on finding and killing the creepy bastard who'd had a field-day playing like a battering ram with my sister, but nobody could do a thing to me for that...

So, why all the attention?

"Hey, you. Hurry!"

"Be right there."

I remembered the gun I'd taken from the woman in Lynn's apartment. That might be it. Maybe she's gone to the police. But that didn't seem such an intelligent thing to do. After she broke into Lynn's place it would have been *me,* not *her,* who would do any complaining—if there was any to *be* done.

For a hurried moment I came close to taking the gun with me. Then I changed my mind. Quickly placing the weapon in the top drawer of my dresser I straightened my shirt, put on a jacket and then walked out to the front room.

"Well, men. Ready to go calling on the Lieutenant."

"Wise guy!" one of them said, shoving me forward. It took all the will power I had to keep from turning and slugging him right where it would do the most good. And that would have gotten me in big trouble, instantly.

The drive to the police station was a study in silence except for the occasional police calls which came over the radio of the squad car. One man sat in back with me, tensely; as if he were afraid that I would open the door and leap out.

But instead, I just sat there, trying to think. My stomach felt like a grinder had been placed inside it and turned on. It was torn to pieces.

I guess I was more nervous than mad. Actually, the escort was just getting me to the station earlier and faster and cheaper than I would have gotten there on my own steam. The only thing was: I didn't know why, in hell, they had come for me, and my two "buddies" didn't seem to be in on the secret. Or, at least, they weren't about to share it with me.

I'd have to wait until I got to the station.

34

Some time ago, the city had given the police department a brand new station at the expense of the taxpayers. It's an impressive place, if you're just looking at it from the outside. Going to it under escort was something different. But I didn't get a chance to see very much of it; and what little chance I got, I didn't use. My mind was thinking about other things.

Questions! And now that I'd had a chance to get over my first shock and surprise, I was, once more, beginning to feel a little pushed out of shape.

I was ushered into a private office. Lt. Johnson was sitting behind a desk. He didn't stand. He just sat there looking at me.

"Have a seat," he offered, after a few long moments. His hand flicked out to indicate a chair opposite his. "Have a few things to ask you about... "

"You mean you got me out of bed just to ask a..."

"Not so fast!" he snapped back. "First, do you want a lawyer?"

Interesting. Usually it was the guy in my position who demanded a lawyer, if that's what was needed – if he was in some way being questioned in a murder case or something. Very strange.

"What for?" I demanded, irritated. "Do I need one?"

"That depends." The man was being evasive.

"Oh, that's just swell! And on what does it depend? "

"How you answer a few questions. But it is my duty to warn you that what you say here will be for the record and you have the right to legal advice and—"

That's when he ran through the standard routine of: *"anything you say can be used against you in a court of law,"* etc. crappolla.

And that was not quite as interesting as I'd have like it to be.

"Yeah, sure, and all the other rot you have to hand out to protect my rights."

"That's the way you guys want it! We don't *make* the laws, we only see to it that they're followed; and they can ham-string us, too."

"My heart goes out to you! What about the bastard

that got at my sister and—"

"Take it easy!" he warned, a little coldly.

"I have a few questions I'd like answers to!" I snapped back.

Johnson stood with a jerking motion. A leap.

"I'll do the questioning, Mr. Matson!" he asserted, slamming one hand on the desktop.

That was one reaction I hadn't quite planned on. A person expects a little sympathy from even the hard-boiled police, when someone in their family has been brutally raped and murdered.

So much more for innocence!

That's when my mind became sharp, instantly on alert. Something was distorted here and I decided that it would be best to play it by ear from then on.

"What did you do last night after you left the morgue?" Johnson inquired, stepping around the desk and sitting on my side of it.

"Drove around," I offered, not seeing any reason for telling him about my little search at Lynn's apartment. It wasn't any of his damn business—anyway, not at this point.

"What else?"

"What do you mean, 'what else'?"

"What else did you do last night?"

"What do you think? What would you do if your sister had been…killed like that?"

"I'm asking the questions!" His eyes were hard and set. "Would you mind answering my question, *from the top?*"

"Well, if you must know, I got loaded and then went home! What would you expect?"

"Nothing else?"

"Nothing!"

"Okay! You said it, I didn't!" He stood and nodded to one of the men who had escorted me in to the station. "You can bring in Mr. Hanson."

"Who's this Mr. Hanson?" I demanded, half rising.

"Sit tight!"

I relaxed. There was no reason for getting all riled up. As it was, I'd already managed to antagonize the lieutenant

36

for no real reason.

The landlord of Lynn's apartment walked in.

"Is that the man?" Johnson asked the manager.

"That's him."

"Thanks. I won't need you for a little while. Just wanted to officially confirm your statement. It might have been somebody else posing as Matson. You can go, for now. Just don't go too far. You'll be at your apartment?"

"Like I said, I spend most of my time there. It's a full-time job."

"Okay. Thanks." Johnson smiled for a moment, and then, after the door closed behind the manager, he faced me, his expression returning to its hard stone. "Now what was that about you saying you went straight home...

"I don't see that it is any of your business."

"Murder is always the policeman's business."

"What do you mean, *murder?*" I cried, standing and feeling every muscle go hard and rigid.

"There was a murdered man found in Miss Matson's apartment. From what the doctor said, he was murdered somewhere between four and six. Does that make things a little clearer to you?"

Numbly, I sat. The blood seemed to be draining from my face. I could hardly believe what he'd said. That put me in the position of the murderer; or at least, a possible suspect.

"Now," he said in a very patient voice, "would you like to start from the beginning?"

"Not particularly. But I guess I have no choice."

"That's just about it!"

I told him everything. From beginning to end. He stopped me at the point where I mentioned the woman. "You have any proof about that?"

I nodded. "Two things. A gun and the license number of her car."

"Why the hell weren't you here earlier?" he demanded.

"Hell, it was early morning and I was tired. And I might point out that I didn't know anything about the murder!"

"That's something that still needs to be proved."

"Who was he?"

"We don't know. At first I thought he might be the man who killed your sister. But we aren't sure."

"Where do I fit in?" I was beginning to get worried. All I needed was a phony murder rap holding me down.

"Right now I'm not quite sure. We won't know until I get a run down on this man."

"What's the guy's name?"

He didn't answer that question. He merely ignored it. "About this license number. You have it? And the gun?"

The number I had in my wallet. I gave it to him. "The gun's at the apartment."

"Where?"

"I can go get it..."

"No, I'll send a man for it."

I told him. There was no point in fighting it. He was the law and what he said, went. The best I could do was to help out all that I could. If I fought him all the way it wouldn't look good for me. And most importantly I wouldn't have a chance of winning. As long as this man didn't know my plans, I at least, had a chance.

"You think this woman had anything to...

"I don't even know if there is a woman," the man pointed out. "That's your alibi. The license number and the gun will either support or destroy your story."

"Swell! Just great! What kind of place are you guys running here?" I demanded, forgetting to be pleasant or quiet. "First my sister gets...well, what happened to her! And now you're accusing me of..."

"Look. This is routine. The apartment manager said that you were up at Miss Matson's rooms. A murder took place there. We bring you in for questioning and you lie like a professional... what are we supposed to think? Especially after last night; you were screaming about getting even and killing the murderer of your sister. Well. This is just a routine checkup!"

That sounded real nice, the way he put things. *Just routine*. Routine routing of Stan Matson into the electric chair.

That was maybe being a little dramatic, but natural

38

thoughts do run through a person's mind when they find themselves in such a mess.

Actually, it would be easy enough to prove that I had no motive for killing the guy. At least I hoped so.

I decided the best thing was to play it straight; be reasonable.

The story I'd told him had to check out. If they couldn't find any connection between me and this man—whoever he might be—then they couldn't pin any charges on me that might stick.

That is, as long as the guy wasn't the rapist. I guess I sat there in the chair for some time before I realized that Johnson had left the room. There was only one exit out of the place and I could see the shadowy form of a man standing outside the door, through the milky glass.

From hunter to murder suspect within a couple of hours. My head was spinning with a million confusing thoughts and questions.

Why had anybody been killed in Lynn's apartment?

What had that tall silver-blonde been doing in her room?

Who was the dead guy?

And what was his connection with Lynn?

Why had she been killed in the first place?

For the first time I was beginning to get the idea that she might have been killed for some reason other than rape. Other than a sex crime. And why should that make any sense?

I don't know how long I sat there in the room, alone, locked in the chamber of my own thoughts. I didn't even get hungry. I paced the floor a lot. But I wasn't really, aware of what I was doing. My mind was like a mad furnace, burning up one possible theory after another. Several facts came out of the combustion of my thoughts and the series of events that had taken place.

Lynn had been killed and raped.

The silver-blonde woman had been looking for something in Lynn's apartment.

A man had been murdered in her apartment.

What connection these three facts might have was

something that I couldn't figure out. At least, not in the confines of the police station.

But they must have some connection. *They had to have!*

The door opened and Lt. Johnson stepped in. "I'm sorry for having kept you waiting for so long, Mr. Matson. But we had a lot of checking to do." His voice was surprisingly pleasant enough. His expression friendly. "You may go."

"What?"

"You may go!"

"I don't get it."

"It's simple. There are no charges to hold you. There's no case. Nothing. I'm letting you go." He spread his hands helplessly. "Do you have any objection to that?"

"Mind telling me a few things?"

"That depends on what you want to know."

"Who's the woman? And who was it that got killed in Lynn's apartment?"

"The man's name was Derk Meechan. There was no way of connecting you with him. You're clear on that."

"The woman?"

"She asked to remain anonymous."

"What the hell!" I couldn't believe my ears. "What are you talking about?"

"She wished to remain unknown. Considering who she was, we didn't see any reason to deny her that wish."

"Damn it all! You mean to tell me that you aren't going to arrest her?"

"She had an iron alibi."

"What the hell are you…"

"That will be all, Mister Matson!"

"But…"

"If you don't mind… I have important matters to take care of. I'm sorry for having kept you so long."

"But I…"

"That'll be all!" His eyes became hard. His expression set.

For a long moment I stared at him and then finally decided I'd better get the hell out while it still was possible.

40

Maybe the thing smelled, but there wasn't any reason I shouldn't take advantage of it. In fact, I realized when I'd gotten outside the station that the thing stank to hell and back! Something was going on that I didn't know anything about. That was obvious. Something, which the lieutenant knew about, but was keeping to himself. He wasn't setting me free without a very good reason. There were more causes for holding me and none that seemed logical for letting me go.

A man had been found dead in an apartment in which I was known to be in at the time.

My "alibi" had one of her own.

I was a perfect target.

Yet he was letting me go without any reason.

Something was damn rotten. Double damn rotten. And I was caught in the middle of the stench.

First, Lynn's death. Now, my own problem. My own trouble. Suddenly I felt like digging a hole and pulling the cover over me.

But, instead, I walked over to a taxi stand, gave the driver of a cab the address of Lynn's apartment and sat nervously on the edge of the back seat, trying to plan exactly how I was going to get information from the manager. And more importantly: just what kind of information I should be looking for.

It seemed like the more I looked; the more I discovered that confused me. First, just a sex crime and a bastard rape artist. Then a silver-blonde woman. A gun. A dead man.

Things seemed to be getting more and more complex by the moment. With me caught in an ever-closing vice. A trap, which I had no way of escaping, if I wanted to find the guy who had killed Lynn. And more. Somebody had murdered a man called Derk Meechan and made it look like it might have been my doing.

Who was the classy silver-blonde woman with so much pull that she could yank herself out of the suspect line?

And the biggest question of all: *Why had Lt. Johnson let me go free?*

MURDER TIMES FOUR, BY CHARLES NUETZEL

☛Chapter Five☚

I stepped out of the cab and walked up to the apartment house where Lynn had lived. I knocked on the manager's office door. He quickly answered. The moment he saw me a flash of terror moved across his face.

"I... mister. Don't..."

"Relax. I'm not the guy who did the killing. Lieutenant Johnson let me out."

"Oh." But he still backed nervously away.

"Can I talk to you for a few moments? I have a couple of questions to ask."

He considered that for a moment, then nodded. "Sure. Come in. Have a seat."

He kept his distance, backing up as I moved forward.

I remained standing.

"What can I do for you?" he asked in a voice that was almost shaking. "I..."

"About Lynn. And the man who was found upstairs in her apartment."

"I didn't know him. He was a stranger. I don't know how he got into the place."

That was just great!

"What about Lynn?"

"Like I told you last night. A nice girl. Had a lot of male friends. Lot of parties. She wasn't noisy. Even the parties were quiet enough."

"Are these apartments furnished or..."

"Hell, no! The people furnish the places themselves."

That was a new item. Expensive furnishings. How could Lynn have afforded it? The implications were suggestive. A lot of men; quite parties. I didn't even want to think about that. "Sure you don't know anybody who Lynn ran around with?"

"Well. You see... I don't make it my business to snoop into my—well, you know how it is."

I nodded. But didn't really know.

"Well…she *did* run around with one of the other tenants. A woman."

"Who?"

"Miss Clifford. They were very close friends. They worked at the same place together."

"Which apartment?"

"I'm not in the habit of giving..."

Reaching into my pocket I pulled out my wallet and picked a couple of bills from it.

His eyes gleamed, greedily. Then after nervously moistening his lips he took the money. "Room 11-A."

"Thanks." I left him without another question or word. His use was over. Finished.

Miss Clifford. 11-A. I knocked. Nobody answered. And I knocked again. A sleepy voice called. I couldn't understand the words. So I knocked once more.

"Oh, wait a minute!" a woman's voice yelled. "Keep your pants on!"

The door opened and an extremely attractive face looked out. Even with the puffy sleep look and the lack of make-up she was more than attractive. Sexy. There was plenty of that.

If the rest of the body followed as well, I couldn't help thinking, helpless to keep from noticing such basics with such a beautifully sexy sight in front of me.

She had sensuous lips. Full. Pink, even without lipstick. Her eyes were large and brown. Her hair brownish-red.

She smiled. It had all the sexy quality of a thousand nude women doing a downright dirty strip show.

"Hello," she greeted in a throaty voice that sent chills down my back. "Who're *you?*"

"Lynn's brother. Can I come in?"

"I'm not dressed decently," she announced, looking at me from head to toe with an up and down movement of her lovely eyes. "But I don't see how that makes so much

44

difference. Do you?"

She opened the door.

"I'm...sick about...Lynn. Sorry about that."

During the next minute we stood in silence. I couldn't get my eyes off her body that was as beautiful as her face. And she wasn't dressed decently. She wore pink panties. The top piece was lightly transparent and to add to the interesting sight, it was loosely half open. One of those little lacy bed jackets that women sometimes wear. On top of this she wore an opened morning robe, which she made no effort to close. Quite a delight to see on such an attractive woman.

Large, bouncing breasts held my attention for a delicious moment.

She laughed when she saw the direction of my gaze.

"Want a drink?" she asked, walking boldly across the room toward a small kitchenette. The lively jerking action of her rounded fanny did things to me that I had no business letting take place. It was as if the woman were either trying to be seductive or merely enjoyed teasing a man.

"This time of the morning?" I asked, not sure if I were referring to the drinking or the sexy way she was moving.

"Why not? Live it up is my motto of life. Live while you can because you don't know what tomorrow will bring!" She laughed again. "I suppose you know what I mean. Considering you're Lynn's brother."

It was a bubbling sound. "So, about that drink?"

"I didn't come for a social call..."

"What dif? So make it social!" she invited. "You just got me out of bed, and the least you can do is...well...whatever!"

She was already pulling out two glasses. "Live a little, brother Stan!"

She laughed again, a giggling sound that moved her breasts.

Ice cubes dropped into the glasses. "I'm sorry, but I don't have anything but whiskey. Okay?"

I gave up. "Okay."

The glasses filled. I started to protest the quantity

when the flow came to a stop. "Soda or water?"

It turned out to be soda and a twist of lemon.

"The lemon makes the difference," she explained, handing me one of the drinks. The smile she gave me as her eyes connected with mine said more than words could ever have said that she was interested in doing more than just sitting around talking and drinking.

Well, I have an ego. Natch. Any male does. And with a lovely little lady like this, under normal circumstances, my thoughts would have raced to home base, driving my body right on target at hers. That's the ego-part. Logic claimed she was quite mad, being so openly seductive with a strange man whom she had invited into her apartment, while so skimpily half-dressed. It was right out of some porno-flick. Not reality.

But her next statement explained something about her actions. Not much, I'll admit, but enough to sooth over any bumpy areas in my mental roadway.

"I've heard a lot about you!" She wiggled her way over to a sofa. Then bounced down onto a cushion. Then she patted the one next to her. "Have a seat."

I stood where I was. I didn't dare get that close to her. There were more important things to do than hit the sack with this dish. As delicious as she appeared to me. Just the thought of enclosing her into my arms was certainly not without its swift response in my body.

"Afraid?" she asked brightly, her eyebrows raising. She smiled again, her lips moving across even white teeth. They parted as she moistened the pink surface of her mouth, making it shine like glass. "I won't bite."

I wasn't so sure of that; or that it wouldn't be one hell of a lot of fun being bitten to death *by her*. In fact, the longer I stood there gazing at her the more overwhelming the temptation became to invite her to strip bite all she wanted.

"Afraid. I might bite back!"

She laughed in a delighted way. "You sound just like I imagined you'd be. Come on over here."

"Like I said: Quite afraid to be that close to you, young lady!" I let it lay there. Took a sip of the drink. It was good. And she was right about the twist of lemon. It helped. I hadn't realized how tense I'd been. Another swallow passed down through my throat.

"Well?" she asked, nervously moving her hand along the full length of her leg.

"I wanted to ask you some questions about Lynn."

Her eyes popped up to mine, suddenly serious. "Sure. Pop away!"

"What happened—what do you know?"

"It was horrible!" Then she shrugged. "Though I'm surprised *she* didn't rape the *man.*" She started to laugh at that, then caught herself. "I'm sorry. It's nothing to kid about, Just that I...well, we were—"

"I know. Good friends." Another gulp of the liquor hit my stomach. "I want to know anything you might be able to tell me about her. What she did. Who she went out with."

"You are her brother!"

"I know that, but you must know we weren't running around together much."

"Yes. But she thought the most of you." Again she smiled that sexy way of hers, once more making her lips shiny and bright and moist. "Lynnie said something about you two being too much alike... or something like that. It all sounded silly as hell to me. After all, like sister like brother!" Her eyes were giving me the up and down routine again. The places where they paused and stopped left no room for guesswork about what she was thinking. It hardly made much sense, considering Lynn's recent death. Hardly the time for seductive escape. Or maybe that was exactly the point.

"I hate to say it," she murmured, raising her fingertips to the top of her thigh, "but I wouldn't mind going out like Lynn.... I don't mean like *that*—but sexed up, you know! To die in orgasm.... If you gotta go.... What a way to go!"

The conversation made me sick.

"I don't think she was feeling..."

"Oh, sure. Sorry. Just that...sex is life. The top of the list for...well, if I have to go I'd pick at the peak of the mountain! So to speak. Sorry if it shocked you. But that's how I am, I suppose."

Oddly enough her words made a perverse logic. This was the kind of woman she was; the kind of person Lynn had become close friends with; and it reflected the world in which it was necessary to walk though in order to find her killer.

And I had to play the game by the rules of those players who came out of the cell-pool of her life.

But this sexy little package of seduction sitting there looking at me was not illusion, but real flesh and blood, quite frankly brazenly flirting with no holds barred. Any normal man would have reacted intensely to the way she was coming on to me. The out-and-out suggestions in her eyes. And the way she wasn't really all that dressed. Yet it didn't seem to bother her in the least.

I'd seen brazen women before in my life, but this one took the medal and highest award.

She was more than just brazen and open about the matter. She was just plain blunt!

"You really shouldn't be so shocked. I can see it in your eyes. But...that's the way I am. And, quite frankly, so was your sister."

She paused, looking down for a moment, then her eyes popped up to mind, once more: "Oh, Lynnie. It's a damn shame. She was a real swinger. Real party giver. You should have come to one of her parties. And the costume blow-out she had New Year's Eve." She giggled. "Only thing was—you had to come in Adam and Eve suits."

I didn't need any more description to get the picture. But she was determined to go into full detail.

"At twelve, all the lights went out and everybody just reached for the nearest..." She laughed again, her hand going to her mouth.

"I'm not interested!" I must have shouted because she jerked and looked shocked. Her eyes had changed from seductive tease to surprise.

"What's with you?" she asked, quite honestly.

I couldn't believe it. She didn't seem to have any idea about the seriousness of the matter. Lynn had been raped and killed. And she didn't realize that this wasn't the time to be making with hot passes. Or idle conversation.

48

"Look. Just do me a favor. *Please?*"

Her lips turned up slightly at the corners. "Okay. Shoot."

She was the bright bubbling personality once more.

"Tell me about Lynn. The people she ran around with."

"Me, for one."

"I know that. That's why I'm here!"

"Well, let me think. There were so many." Her fingers were working on the tiny little ribbon that held the top piece of her bed jacket together.

"You know about a woman? A silver-blonde. Tall. Regal-looking. High society."

"Oh, sure! That's Theresa." Her voice began to get a sharp edge on it. A cutting sound. "That De Bray woman! Bitch! Thinks she's so great! Just because she legally shacked up with a rich man. *She's just a little whore!*" Her eyes sparkled again, changing the expression on her face. "But who wants to talk about that witch!"

The ribbon pulled loose. The bed jacket parted.

My eyes were frozen on the lovely sight. It would have been hard for anybody to keep from looking. "Why talk about other women when I'm here?"

"Good Christ!" was all that I could say. I felt nauseated. Heated. Fiery and disgusted. Bewitched. Bothered like all of Hell's fires had been built under me. And down right guilty. I wanted to simply jump her and ravish that wanton body.

"Damn it all!" I cursed loudly, unable to move. "What the hell are you doing?"

"What do you think, Brother Stan?" she laughed in a low, rasping voice. She stood and started gliding over in my direction.

The sight was one of the most disgustingly delightful things I'd ever seen. Disgusting only because it was completely out of place. This was not the time for such things; yet this girl didn't seem to realize it. Or care. Her mind was filled with only one thought.

"Sister Lynn told me a lot about you. She said you loved women like me. That you were big and strong. And that you knew all about how to treat a girl right. How to make her like it!"

Now she was standing within inches of me. I hadn't been able to move from the spot. The little jerking sway of her hips as she had made each movement forward had held me captive as if I were hypnotized. It seemed almost as if I was under some kind of physical "spell." Literally drugged by the site of this lovely, seductive sexual treat. Which could hardly be thought of as being abnormal, under the conditions.

I *was* tired. The drink was working on my body. This young woman was racing my blood cells into a frantic dizzy course through my veins.

"You got little old me. *Here!* You don't really want to talk about other things, do you?" Her hands slid around my neck, cupping it with her fingers. "You don't want to run away, do you?"

I discovered that it was impossible to move from the spot even if I'd wanted to. I felt as if some drug held me captive and helpless.

Her body touched mine. Her voice whispered almost breathlessly. "You'll do fine. Just fine! Oh, yes, you'll do just wonderfully!"

Taking hold of my hand she urged me toward the bedroom.

It was like a dream. A drugged dream that seemed to never end. A delightful dream of ecstasy.

I felt soft warm flesh under my hands, moist lips surrounding me, and the hammering clutch of legs tightly clasped about my body in a savage embrace as jungle drums pounded with every thrusting movement! It was a universe of sensation that blurred, shifted, to become a distant dark black cloud of almost agonizing ecstasy.

Slowly, I was drawn into a bottomless well of red exhaustion that gently closed in around me until the world of reality slid away into a cold, restless black sleep.

Then I remembered where I was...

What the hell had I done? That was the first mental reaction.

The dirty, little wanton!

I felt almost numb, in a half-conscious state, not able to completely regain consciousness.

The bitch must have drugged me with the very sight of her lovely body. That, and the liquor. It was the only explanation. That wonderfully, delightfully over-sexed female had seduced me with a drink and a body out of hell.

Just the thought of her trembling, gasping, and straining against me sent hot fire up my spine. Whatever she had done was, beyond any question, fantastic. Under any other circumstances I would have wanted to spend a month of joy-making with such a woman.

My head throbbed.

I looked in the bed next to me.

She was gone.

I rolled over, dazed, curled up into a ball, suddenly sobbing at the memory of what had happened to Lynn, my dear little kid-sister.

My mind and brain were swimming in some kind of bubbling numbness, which slowly closed in around all thoughts as I embraced its wonderful seductive escape.

MURDER TIMES FOUR, BY CHARLES NUETZEL

☙Chapter Six☙

I woke up with a headache. It was a throbbing pain. At first I didn't know where I was. I had the feeling of uneasiness. Of something wrong or out of place. Maybe it was the feel of the bed under me. It seemed alien. It's funny how even a bed can have a very familiar or unfamiliar feel about it. You get used to one and another seems quite different and strange.

This was a strange bed.

I remembered a body screaming in happy delight. It was a foggy remembrance: As if out of some fantastic dream-movie.

I started to call, "Miss Clifford," but decided it would be rather silly calling her by that name, after what just happened between us.

It sounded too formal.

The perverted bitch!

To hell with formality! my mind argued back. "Miss Clifford?"

No answer.

I called again. Still there was no answer. The third time I accented the words by getting painfully out of bed.

Silence was my answer.

Walking from the bedroom I looked through the apartment. She was nowhere in sight.

Never had my head ached so much. I needed a drink. My mouth was dry.

Walking over to the small kitchenette I reached for the bottle from which she had poured the drinks earlier. How much earlier? I didn't know.

My fingers wrapped around the bottle. Then they released it. A thought was hammering in the back of my head, keeping rhythm with the throbbing beat of the stabbing ache at my temples. *I'd gone to her like a lamb to slaughter. Why?*

Like a drugged man I had no will over myself. Only one thought had built in my mind and that had been to take her in my arms and relieve the ache that had started inside me. Then I'd felt those lovely arms around me. The sound of her breath had been agonized in my ears.

The little bitch had seduced me like Grant had taken Richmond. I hadn't had a thing to say about it. And that's what was bothering me. I *hadn't* had anything to say about it. The timing was wrong. I didn't even know the girl. The place might have been right—but it wasn't the right time... That, alone, would have stopped me from being interested in any "seduction party."

Yet, there it was. I'd gone right ahead and done it. Drugged. Drugged by her sensual beauty. Her brazen conversation. Her open and demanding invitation. Her forceful seductive power. Literally taken by the hand. Been drugged by her!

Drugged!

That word stood out and suddenly I realized that was what had been hammering at my subconscious mind for some moments now. The little sexy bitch had downright drugged me. She must have. It was the only logical explanation. No other reasoning made sense. And even this didn't make sane sense. What was her motive?

I'd seen plenty of beautiful nude women in my life. One time or another they'd acted much the same way she had.

Barbara was as wildly demanding as any woman could get—yet, I could pull away from her to answer the phone. So it didn't figure.

But if I were drugged, that would add up.

The front door opened and in bounced Miss Clifford. Completely dressed in a tight fitting skirt and an even tighter fitting red sweater.

"Hello there, Brother Stan!" she greeted as if nothing unusual had happened; as if what *had* taken place was an everyday occurrence between us. As if we were lovers or married or just rooming together.

"What the hell did you put into my drink?"

"I'll never tell!" She winked playfully.

"You did, then?"

"Natch! What else?" She flashed by me and put the armful of groceries on the sink. "You're a man and I'm a woman and I wanted to do what comes naturally. So... a little something to get things started. Nursie things. At the hospital where I work...if you know what, when and where...isn't difficult to get what you need. A doctor here and a doctor there and guess what? They'll do just about anything I ask of them. We nurses can get into a lot of stuff all you other folks can't imagine even exists! And as for you...well, I always wondered about Lynnie's brother! After all, you're kinda famous. Well, within the circle of friends she had, anyway!"

I couldn't believe my ears. I'd been a total stranger.

"Doesn't it matter that we didn't even know each other?" I managed to gulp out.

"Why? Lynnie told me all about you. I was fairly burning myself up to know you and get with it. You seemed just like an old friend. Anyway... I heard that you weren't against picking up girls! That you were a swingin' hot jock!"

"That's different!"

"Why?"

I ignored the question. The whole conversation was completely out of context with what I'd come up to talk to her about.

I noticed her eyes were looking rather pointedly at me. That's when I realized I didn't have anything on. But I wasn't in any mood to let that stop me. Right at that moment I felt like beating the hell out of her. "Don't you have any idea how I feel about Lynn?"

She shrugged. "So, what can you do about it? Stop living? People die every day, I can vouch for that. As a nurse I see a lot of death. You gotta keep living, honey. Other wise, what's the point?"

"God, how I'd like to beat your rotten brains in!" I cursed in fury, finding it hard to control my now raging temper.

"Oh, how delightful. You sure know how to turn a gal on, right from warm to burning hot. Keep that up and I'll give you a second run!" Her eyes lighted. "And that sure would be nice!"

"Okay! Okay! Okay!" was all I could say. Walking away from her and toward the bedroom I heard her laughing happily, as if at some sidesplitting joke.

"Be careful," she called in a teasing voice. "I might come in there and take your manly charms once more into my...oh, I better not think about that!"

"Just stay where you are!" I demanded, rather angrily.

"Gee, don't get angry at me. Tain't my fault that you're such a hard man to turn down! And once I get my claws on a guy, well, you know how good it can be. I keep all my lovers really happy. I'm a bitchy and possessive lay-dee!" She laughed at that. "Well, once I get 'em I don't let go if they're as good as you are! I want 'em day and night, all night and all day. Just hankerin' to do me in. Now, is that wrong? Really? Ya gotta live while you can. Make the most of it. Gather the roses while they're lush and beautiful."

She continued to talk from the other room: "I'm sorta crazy about a male bod. And oh, I get to see a lot of them at work. They don't know it, but...a nurse can see so much when they are unconscious. I know, I'm naughty, but I can't help myself. And it doesn't hurt anybody. I kinda get all shaky in side, all over, just at the thought of having a man all over me...you were great, hon. Really enjoyed you. Could totally go for...a lot more of what we sampled...oh well."

She rattled on like that, but I wasn't daring to pay any attention to her words. They were rather suggestive to my male hormones, which just wanted to bounce around like little flaky cells in heat to bake every nerve in my body to instant alert.

One thing I'd come to a conclusion about: she was some kind of nut or something. A complete emotional screwball. And the quicker I got out of the place the better I'd feel. I had gotten what I wanted. Information. And that's all that really counted. This girl didn't mean anything to me. She was just a little tramp and easy make-job for the first and any man that came along. Hot sex. And that was one thing I didn't need to tamper with—not at that moment, anyway. I'd met quite a few in my time; not as crazy as this one, but they weren't too hard to find.

All I could think of was getting out and never coming back. The whole scene disgusted me. Delightful sex-package, that Miss Clifford might be! But there was something really odd about her attitude, as if not wanting to let go, not wanting to stop, not releasing a man once she had her hooks in him.

Actually I was a bit angry with her.

For two good reasons. One, because of the time she had cost me. And the other had to do with my sister. To think that she'd run around with such a bitch in heat.

Logical? Hell no! I'd known a lot of such delightful women in my life—some seedy, some just delicious in every way. But swingin' ladies all.

And the New Year's Eve party she'd told me about.

Not sister Lynn, my mind protested, violently. *Not little sister Lynn!*

I got dressed and by the time I returned to the living room Miss Clifford was sitting on the sofa with a drink in her hand, another on the table in front of her.

"Why'd you get all dressed up?" she asked with a funny expression on her face. Her finger started to pull at the bottom of her skirt. "I thought we might start another little wing-ding."

"You go wing-ding yourself!"

"But... I planned we'd really—"

"Go fly a kite and cool off!" I moved toward the door. I didn't even want to talk to her any more. There were more important things to take care of that didn't have anything to do with "wing-dinging."

"Ah, but Brother Stan," she cried, running forward and getting between the door and me. "I thought you liked little old Linda in bed. Wasn't I good enough? I can be better. Oh, you don't know how better I can be, honey bunny!"

I felt a hard lump of acid cough up through my throat. It seemed incredible. "Miss Clifford..."

"Oh, you can call me Linda, all things considered!

After all, we're intimate friends. Well, at least some intimate parts of our bodies are as friendly as they could get … oh, I'd like to get them together again!" she announced in a silky low voice, putting her arms around me and squeezing herself tightly against my back. "Come on, let's have a party!"

"Christ!" I violently pushed away from her. She gave a sigh of excitement and moved closer again, attempting to grab hold of my clothes.

"Damn it all, *let go!*" I yelled, struggling to move away and at the same time open the door.

She was bubbling with happy laughter. "Come on! Come on, *Big Boy!*" she screamed. "That's the way! Fight! Struggle! Oh, yes. Do battle with me. Be deliciously power-ful. Take me in those big, juicy hard arms of yours. Let me feel all your hardness all over me. Oh, yes…force me be-yond my well to resist!"

For a moment I stood there frozen with surprised shock. *She was enjoying herself!* The instant my struggles stopped she started to pull off her sweater.

I didn't wait to see any more. Before she completed the act I was on my way down the hall.

But she came running out after me, her sweater half off. "Come on back. Please. Oh, *please!*"

She had the sense to call quietly. All we needed were people coming out of their apartments and seeing this mad display. We'd find ourselves in the police station before we knew what hit us.

The only thing that stopped me from turning and slapping her a hard one across the face was the fact that I re-alized that I would have been doing exactly what she liked best. In fact any rough thing that a man might do to her was a turn-on.

Her hand clutched my jacket and I turned, stopped and looked directly at her. Cold. "Would you mind going to hell?"

Her expression changed. For a long moment she looked blankly at me. Then the features of her face distorted terribly. Her appearance became suddenly ugly.

"You bastard! You damned fairy! Some of the men at work are better than you! A dead body. A friggin' dead

58

body. And I've seen enough of them as a nurse! You're no good, anyway. No good at all! Nothing. I've known men half your size that had better and..."

I didn't hear the rest. She was screaming at the top of her lungs. Insanely. Her fists had come to rest on her hips and she stood there in the hall, legs spread slightly, with only a bra and skirt on, shouting curses and calling me names. I didn't even bother to listen.

My head was still throbbing from the after effect of the drug she had given me. I was inwardly nauseated. That might have been caused by the emotional reaction to Linda Clifford or from the drugs. Or nerves. Or a little of all that.

There was no way of knowing.

All I was aware of was that I wanted to get away from her; from the apartment.

At least I'd gained something. The name of the silver-blonde. And that was a blessing. It was almost worth it.

Theresa De Bray. The next stop in my search. Maybe the last. I didn't have any way of knowing.

First I had to get a cab to take me to my own apartment. There I could look up the DeBray address in the phone book. And then drive over to see my silver-blonde-haired lead.

At the corner I found a public phone behind a gas station. Five minutes later a cab arrived.

Another ten minutes and I was walking down the hallway, which led to my three-room apartment. When I came opposite the door I saw light shining under the door jam and the sound of a progressive jazz combo playing.

Opening the door I walked in, not knowing exactly what to expect. The only thing I *did* know was that whatever was in the room was big trouble. It *had* to be. It was.

Barbara Blair. In a slinky, tight-fitting red dress. The V-neckline accented the full, rounded curve of her pointed breasts. I didn't need a second look to know what she had in mind; or to make myself want to turn around and walk out. But it was already too late to do that.

"Hi there, Stanny-boy," she greeted happily, running forward and flinging her arms around my neck. As her body pressed eagerly against mine, she added: "I thought you weren't ever going to get home. I have dinner half fixed. Cocktails. I thought you'd need a woman to tell your sorrows to. Some comfort and tender loving care."

That's all I needed. For some reason women didn't seem to understand the basic facts of life. Like a man sometimes wants to be left alone. A man sometimes has other things more important to do than hitting the sack. Like find the rape artist.

How could I tell Barbara that I wasn't in the mood for her or anybody like her? That I was tired, weary, anxious to continue a search for a man I planned on killing.

"I thought it'd be a nice surprise for you!" she continued to chatter, moving back and giving me a knowing look.

"It's a surprise, all right," I sighed tiredly. *What could I say?*

The food smelled good, though. It made me realize that I was hungry. In fact, I remembered I hadn't eaten since the day before. That was a very good reason to be hungry.

"Why don't you take a shower?" she suggested, "and get into something more comfortable, while I fix dinner?"

I just nodded silently. I could use a shower.

I could use a good meal. And a little time to find a way to let her know that her plans would end after the dinner part had been finished. Tell her to go home like a nice girl and let me carry on with my own activities.

There was one point that did present itself to me then: *things weren't in such a hurry that I couldn't afford a little time for a shower and some food.*

They weren't—yet!

☛Chapter Seven☚

The shower was great. The dinner was even better. I'd made it a point to be fully dressed in street clothes before coming out of the bedroom to subtly prepare Barbara for the basic fact that we weren't about to have after dinner fun and games.

Her only reaction at seeing me was to take a fast double look. Then her lips smiled sweetly and she brought over my cocktail shaker.

"Martinis."

"Good!"

For a long time the two of us stood in the center of the room, just sipping the drinks and looking at each other.

One thing that I could say about Barbara; she had a certain genuine class about her. Not too tall, but tall enough to fit perfectly against a man my height. She was the kind of woman a person didn't mind flashing around; in fact, a man would go out of his way to show her off.

Class. Intelligence.

What surprised me was that she didn't attempt to make any passes or suggestions of playing around. She was riding with the punches.

"I'm sorry about last night," I apologized.

She moved her head quickly from side to side. "Don't. It was horrible!"

I shrugged.

I didn't really want to think about what had taken place, in that way. I managed to keep in focus only the fact I had to get the guy who did it. I didn't have any energy to feel sick or sad or over-emotional in a self-pity way. And anyway, I'd always felt that grief was only for the living, not the dead. If there is an after life, then there should be joy for the person who has passed on; they had progressed, taken the next step. If death is truly the end of the personality, then why feel terrible grief? The dead person doesn't know anything any more; they feel nothing; they have no awareness of what has taken place—they have just stopped being! So, from my point of view, grief has always been only for the living. For yourself, because of what you lost; and a little because you know others expect you to react in that way. Show-biz time!

It was a nice theory on paper. But it didn't work too well in real life. The only way I could bypass grief was simply focusing on the man I planned on killing. My total acceptance of this was strangely without real emotion; it was simply something I felt necessary to do.

The drinks finished, we sat down to dinner. Plain old dinner. Simple. Effective. Great! Steaks as only Barbara could cook them. And all the trimmings. That was another point I had to give her. She could cook like nobody I'd ever known. And I consider myself an expert on such matters.

Afterwards I looked across at Barbara. She gave me that sweet smile of hers.

"I know," she said, an edge of regret in her voice, "you have plans."

I nodded. What could I really say? Great dinner? Gotta leave now? Sorry, kid?

I stood and walked over to the telephone where the directory was. Picking it up I looked for the name DeBray. As I had feared, it wasn't listed.

I turned to the phone. Dialed information. Asked for the number of Theresa DeBray.

Luck, for the first time, was with me. But they wouldn't give me the address. Which helped one hell of a lot! But it did tell me one thing. Her phone was listed. It also told me that her home was some place in Bel Air. All I had to do was go to Bel Air, step into a phone booth and look up the number there. That would give the address. It would just be a matter of leg work. Perhaps.

Barbara was standing quite close to me when I looked up.

"Anything I can help you with?" she asked in an almost gentle way.

"No. I have to take care of this..."

"Okay. I'll clean up here."

"No, don't be silly. I'll take care of..."

"I *want* to."

I shrugged. There wasn't the time or energy left to argue. So I let her do anything she wanted to. There were more important things for me to take care of right then.

"I'm terribly sorry. It's a hell of a thing for me to do... run off like this!"

She just bit her lower lip. Her eyes looked tenderly sad. But she didn't say anything.

I stood and gently reached for Barbara, slowly drawing her form tightly to me. The kiss was quick and more tender than any before then. Her lips were padded silk. Just a quick touch, but still pleasant enough.

Then I walked out. I knew she'd have the place cleaned like new by the time I got to the DeBray house. She was that way. Neat. Clean. Careful. Once this thing was over, I promised myself, I would take Barbara into some hideaway for the duration—if that were still possible.

It was only a fifteen-minute drive to Bel Air. A matter of a minute to look up the DeBray address in the telephone directory. Another five to find her house. It was a huge place. Two story. A massive structure. From what Linda Clifford had said, Theresa DeBray married into a *really* rich set-up.

So what was her connection with Lynn? And what had she been doing in Lynn's apartment? It didn't add up. Not at all.

I parked the car. Then walked the expanse of the pathway that cut through the large green lawn toward the huge wooden double door entrance. I rang the doorbell a moment later.

A small, thin butler opened the door.

"Yes?" he asked, as if to say, *who, the hell, are you?*

"Is Mrs. DeBray in?"

"Who's calling?"

"Just tell her it's Stan Matson, Lynn Matson's

brother!" I ordered, pushing forward. He tried to block my way but it took only a slight shove to move past him.

"Sir!" The man turned toward me. His face was white with stiff-necked shock. "I'll have you know that this is a private residence!"

"Keep it!"

"What?"

"Just go get Mrs. DeBray!"

"Sir?" He just stood there looking stupidly at me. He was apparently used to taking orders, but not from a stranger.

"Mrs. DeBray!"

He hesitated, not knowing what to do. The poor guy looked like a shriveled baby elephant, swaying its trunk from side to side, not knowing which direction to turn. Frightened; thin and confused.

"What is it, Ben?" I heard Theresa's calm voice call from another room.

"Madam, there's a man here who's forced his way into..." I had started to move toward the room from where I'd heard the woman's voice. He shuffled after me. "You can't go in there!"

"Take it easy little man," I ordered while gently as possible brushing him aside, out of my way.

The room that I found myself looking into, a moment later, was a large study-like place. All the walls were lined with bookcases. In the corner was a large built-in color television. Several pieces of heavy furniture were placed a couple of feet from the bookcases, all facing inwards, toward a huge oak desk. Everything was neat and orderly, except one chair, one cigarette stand—and one woman.

A change had taken place in Theresa DeBray. She wore tight slacks and a loose-fitting man's shirt with the top button open. Her hair was down, straight, over her shoulders. The lipstick that she wore was dark red and much fuller in shape, making her lips look more sensual and soft.

When she saw me she jumped to her feet, the drink in her hands almost spilling on the rug. Her eyes became large and wide with shock. "What's the idea of..."

"Break it off! I don't think you have to play this phony act with me any more!" I announced, stepping forward into the center of the room. "I think we have a few things to talk about."

Her expression relaxed after that. Then she smiled. It was calculated. I was taken aback at the change, at the sensual dignity of that turning up of her lips; it was completely different from the woman I'd met in Lynn's apartment the night before. Of course the slacks and shirt helped a lot in causing the changed effect. She was now just a young girl with a rather unusually attractive body. Round and brimming. Not as tall. Not as regal. Just a sexy number. I was beginning to wonder if maybe Linda Clifford hadn't been right in calling her a "witch" and whore. It might fit quite perfectly.

Then suddenly she straightened to her full height and the change was amazing. The regal, high society woman. Even with the slacks and shirt she had suddenly taken on the classy superior appearance.

"Ben, you can leave us," she told the butler, in that clipped tone of authority.

The man left, slightly dazed, closing the door behind him.

I was a bit bewildered myself now. Theresa DeBray was turning out to be a complicated woman. A woman of many charms, and different sides. Right now her attitude changed slightly once more. It relaxed a bit. The superiority left, but not the regal look.

"Well," she sighed tiredly, "I guess you want a few answers."

That was putting things a little simply: *I wanted plenty of answers.*

She walked over to a small cabinet and opened the double doors. It was a complete bar supplied with everything from ice to liquor. "What'll you have?"

I wasn't really in the mood to be drinking. I wanted answers to a lot of questions, which only this woman could give. But since she was making this attempt to be friendly, I decided it would be better to take her offer. "Make it scotch."

"Rocks, straight, soda or water?" she asked, picking out a glass and pausing with her hand over the ice bucket.

"Ice and soda."

A moment later I had a drink in my hands. The scotch was good. More than just good; and obviously very expensive. Like the woman.

She was now sitting in the chair that she'd been occupying when I had barged in on her. "Make yourself comfortable."

I remained standing. Maybe it was childish, but it made me feel a sense of command being able to look down on this young woman who was the mistress of all these surroundings. Looking down gave me that sense of superiority, which, for some reason, I seemed to need.

"Where do you want me to start?" she asked, briefly looking directly into my eyes. She must have noticed my unconscious attraction to the top of her half-open shirt for her fingers absently buttoned it closed.

"From the beginning. How you happened to be in Lynn's apartment. Where you met her. What connection is there between you and her. And her death!"

She started at that, as if shocked by an electric jolt. Then she nervously took a deep breath. "What... what do you mean—about her death...? I mean, *what* connection *could* I have?" She was on the defensive; and abruptly realized how it made her sound and look. "It's not that there *is* any connection, of course. Just that you startled me."

I let it go at that.

"About Lynn."

"What about her?"

"You must have known her."

"Oh, sure. We roomed together for a couple of months. Before I met Victor."

"Your husband?"

"You see, he was older... and well, he took a liking to me... and..."

"Okay." I wasn't interested in the story of her life. All I wanted to know was about her connection with Lynn. "What about the dead man? Derk Meechan?"

Just ever so slightly her body tensed. Then she relaxed. "I don't know anything about him."

"Who was in the car with you last night?"

"I don't see how that has anything to do with you!"

66

she snapped, suddenly standing. "I believe that you are going just too far. The only reason I decided to be nice at all was because I felt sorry for you. Your sister last night and then that murder which... well the police still aren't convinced that you didn't do it...and...well, I thought maybe I could help you... *But you are going just too far!"*

Somewhere along the line I had hit pay dirt. That much I knew.

"Look," I fairly shouted back at her. She retreated slightly. "I've had just about enough from you!"

For a long moment she stood there, white and quiet. "I don't have to take that kind of crap from anybody!" she screamed, suddenly, taking a step toward me. "You get the hell out of here!"

The swearing coming from such a woman as Theresa DeBray was an unexpected jolt. I'd be able to picture a lot of women laying into a person in that way, but it was surprising to see Theresa storming up like that.

"I'm not leaving until I get a few more facts!"

"You're leaving right now; or I'll call the police!" She stood there before me, her fists on her hips. Suddenly she looked small and helpless. Like a little child, defying its parent.

"Just calm down!" I ordered in a softer voice.

"Are you going to leave?"

"Not until..."

She moved toward the phone. I jumped after her, taking hold of her shoulder.

The physical contact was jolting electricity.

Never had that happened to me. I'd heard about people touching and getting an electric shock, but this was the real thing. It was unbelievable.

She had felt it, too. The reaction caused her to turn in my direction. Her eyes were frowning; puzzled. We stood there looking at each other for a long time; neither able to understand what had taken place.

That contact. That one touch. The silky, delightful feel of her shoulder under the cloth of the shirt.

In those moments, looking at her, I became aware of another shock.

The scent of perfume; light and delicate.

My own mouth was slightly dry. The blood began to move through me, a little faster. My breathing felt a bit heavy.

She started to turn toward the phone again. Reach out for it.

I moved to stop her. My fingers clasped around her wrist. That shock jolted right up through my arm. I felt the same reaction in her arm, where my fingers were touching her wrist. We both turned once more toward each other. Her mouth dropped open helplessly. Neither of us said anything. I didn't know exactly what to do or say.

My body was automatically crying to sweep her up in my arms and thrill fully to that new sensation. Strip her naked and ravish the hell out of her. My mind was the only thing that kept me from doing just that. From the expression on her face I could tell that similar thoughts were rushing through her brain.

Suddenly, all interest in everything else slid away from me. I found only one emotion rattling around in every cell of my body and mind. Whirling like an insane storm.

Confusion! I couldn't think about anything. All that I was aware of was the pulse of her so close, so lovely, so hot and wanting.

The touch of her. The feel of her where my hand was still holding her wrist.

Then, slowly, my fingers relaxed their hold. My arm slipped down to my side. Without another word I turned and walked out.

I don't even remember having moved through the hallway or out the front door or across the lawn to my car. The next thing that I was consciously aware of was driving along the freeway toward my apartment.

Never had anything ever affected me in such a strange way. Never had I felt such a raw physical or emotional reaction toward a woman. One moment both of us at each other's throats and just because of one physical contact we had been jarred to the core; numbed senseless.

I could have easily taken her. Never had anybody shocked me in this way before. And, actually, she hadn't

68

done a thing. But I knew she would not have resisted – in fact the woman might have aggressively devoured me in the same way that I wanted to totally feast on her flesh.

I was hardly aware of driving. Or having brought the car to a stop at my apartment. Or walking up the steps, opening the door to my rooms. I was just emotionally and mentally and physically drained of all energy. I couldn't even think about anything but the demanding necessity for release of all those pent-up mental and physical reactions that had been caused by that one contact with Theresa DeBray.

As I closed the door behind me I heard a happy cry of delight.

Barbara!

The first reaction was: *What the hell was she still doing here?*

The second was a sense of numbing relief.

Suddenly I wanted to just fall into her arms, have her comfort me, enclose me, let me smother myself against her, to find some release from all the pain which had drown around my very existence in the last hours. It had nothing to do with sex and everything to do with just that. And much more, a longing to be feel close to the woman herself.

I literally wanted Barbara in ways I'd never imagined possible before that moment. It was as if she were some kind of safe heaven into which I might find peace.

Murder Times Four, by Charles Nuetzel

☛Chapter Eight☚

Looking back later, when all the events could be viewed with an unemotional and more impersonal slant, it seemed like a fantastic set of events that happened in so short a span of time. In the first place, women don't normally fall at my feet from every direction. They have a tendency to view me rather neutrally, like any other bachelor who runs around like I do. It so happened that Barbara and I were on our way to a really swinging affair that had been cut short before it had really begun in full swing. As for Linda Clifford, she was an exception; one of those maybe once a lifetime experiences—if he's not lucky to escape from it! And then there was Theresa DeBray. That was definitely something for the books. *Electric sparks!* Two fission-loaded particles making contact.

It wasn't abnormal that Barbara *would* be waiting for me. The buildup had started some time ago. She was fired up almost to the point of no return the evening before and then cut off so suddenly by that shocking phone call.

The only thing is; I should have been looking for a rape artist, not making the scene with a woman.

But people don't act intelligently all the time. Their actions are not always rational. My mind wasn't even rational. Just the sight of Barbara made me want to rip the dress off her.

She was stretched out on the sofa when I closed the door behind me. Her voice was a shock. It knocked my mind into the present reality.

"Stanny-boy!" she greeted. One look was all I needed to see that she was slightly drunk. Which made Barbara even more sensually inclined. As if she needed any help. A second

71

look showed me that she was high enough not to really be aware of anything outside of the direct object of her attention.

Right now all her attention was on me. And the smile she gave did nothing to cause me to have any doubt that her desires were directed on only one object and destination.

I stood there, leaning on the door, looking at her. For a long moment I was too dazed to really be thinking straight. I watched as she opened her mouth and moistened her lips. Then a hand went to the top of her dress. It was one of those affairs, which opened from the top. Slowly, button by button, she started pulling it away from her body.

Her breathing was heavy. Her bra was straining to hold back her breasts from bursting outwards; seemed like it was fighting a losing battle.

All this time her eyes were locked to mine. It was as if we were carrying on a mental conversation. And the conversation was a continuation of what had started at the beach house. She was simply saying, *My virgin is hot, take it from me! It's all yours!*

At first I couldn't move. Then the daze slowly began to clear and I stepped across the room. It was the longest walk I ever took. It seemed to take forever. Time was standing still between each step.

"Help me," she cried, almost desperately, churning on the sofa in her frantic attempts to get out of the bra.

Then suddenly I wasn't even thinking about Theresa DeBray. Barbara had every bit of my attention from the moment I'd felt her arch up against me.

There's nothing like a good woman giving a man her greatest gift at the right time. Even if her "virgin" wasn't! Well... hot. Yes. But Barbara was no where near a virgin! Thank all the Gods! Maybe it didn't make sense downing myself in her arms at that moment, yet as it was probably the best thing that could have happened.

The mind can take only so much emotional strain and then it needs a real escape, real rest. And sanity.

"Oh," she sighed as I was smothered against her shoulder. "I...oh, Stan."

I wanted to say something to her, make some sound

of appreciation, but my lips were fully occupied in simply worshipping her flesh, from shoulders to breasts, all the way down across her flat belly and at last into the very heart of her greedy passions, as she clutched me to her, sobbing in joy. She arched up against my kisses, fingers tensely caressing the back of my neck.

Then suddenly I felt her arched back, and she merely sobbed: "Oh…don't wait!"

Just that and we shifted so skillfully, as only two experienced lovers can. Our bodies found each other with wild, driving force that was totally overwhelming. It was, by then, more take than give on both of our parts. We were like two savage beasts grabbing at one another after a long famine, frantic, hungry to devour away the almost anguished need bursting throughout our bodies.

Barbara totally exhausted me within her loving embrace, but not until both of us had made such demands that nothing was left but dark rest. Wonder release closed about my thoughts, flooding over consciousness like a gigantic wave, numbing all nerves and worries in soothing sleep.

Out of that relaxed and contented and fulfilled sense of well-being, my mind started floating upwards, as if it were a thing of material substance working its way toward the surface of a gigantic ocean. As the thoughts finally began to surface, they added idea to idea, concept to concept, question to question, until I sat bolt upright, almost sending Barbara spinning to the floor.

A sense of reality had abruptly shattered the fantasy. What was I doing here, when I should be out looking for the man who had raped and killed my sister?

Without a word to Barbara, I got dressed. Fixed coffee and, after shaving, sat down to drink a cup of the black brew.

Barbara was dressed too, now. She sat opposite me, looking into another cup. For a long time we were both silent and then she looked up into my eyes.

"Want to tell me what you've been running around and chasing your tail for?" she asked. Her face was frowning. She looked concerned. Honestly interested.

I just shook my head, silently, from side to side. 1

didn't really want to tell her but I realized that she deserved some explanation.

She'd been a real sport in more than one way.

The weekend shot to hell.

If anybody deserved an explanation, it was Barbara. But I didn't really know if I could tell her the truth; at least, not the whole truth.

"I've been trying to find Lynn's killer."

She nodded, as if to say that's what she figured. "Found out anything?"

"I don't know. I just don't know." I guess I was talking more to myself than Barbara.

One thing that I simply loved her for was not lecturing me about leaving all that to the police. I guess she was simply too smart to play the game that way. Nothing that she, nor anybody else, could say would have diverted me from my self-defined mission. And Barbara knew that to be a very hard fact around which neither of us could move.

It seemed that I'd been running around in circles. From one woman to another. It didn't make sense, when I looked at it that way.

But from the viewpoint of what I'd discovered about Lynn, it might make a lot of sense.

First: Lynn—as much as I hated to admit—had been something of an arty tramp.

Giving sex parties. Apparently not caring who got to her. If Linda Clifford and the DeBray girl were any indication of what Lynn had been like, well...

It made me sick to realize that my sister was nothing but a cheap quick-job in bed.

Maybe not so cheap, considering her apartment furnishing. Maybe rather expensive.

Second: There was some connection between Lynn, Theresa DeBray and the murdered man in her apartment. What that connection might be, I didn't know.

Third: There was, in some way, a connection between Theresa DeBray and what she had been looking for in Lynn's apartment and the murder of Lynn. What that might be was anybody's wild guess.

Of course, I was drawing theories from mere hints.

Like Theresa's reaction to some of the questions. Her anger. Her side-stepping. Hints that weren't conclusive.

"What happens now?" Barbara asked, interrupting my thoughts.

"That's a good question. A damn good question." I stood, then, and looked down at her. After a moment's silence I said: "I hate to do this, but..."

"You have to leave?" she finished, smiling and standing. "I know. Sure wish it was otherwise."

I nodded, feeling cheap and selfish, yet unable to do anything about it.

"Don't worry in the least. I have to get home anyway. Things to take care of...things."

Her voice faded out and she knew I realized that she'd been lying through her teeth. "No, that's not true. I'd rather spend the day in your arms!"

I felt suddenly sorry for her. More than that, actually. A bit tender. Gently, I reached for her. Drew her close. The firm but not insistent pressure of her body, as it fitted tight against mine, was almost a heavenly feeling. Her lips were salty and sweet-tasting, all at once. It was one of those tender moments that sometimes connects two people.

"Thanks," I said, stepping away. "Thanks. For everything."

"Don't think anything about it." She shrugged sadly.

"I mean it, though. You're a real sport!"

"A real sport," she sighed. The tone seemed to have a bitter knot in it.

"A real sport," she repeated. "That's me!"

"Thanks for being...you!" My voice was thick with real emotion. "I mean that."

"I mean it, too," she murmured softly. "I mean it, too."

Whatever that meant, I had no real idea.

I was already on my way out. She'd take care of herself. Her own car would be nearby. And, anyway, I didn't have the time now. No time for anything. It was as if that brief interlude with Barbara had cleared away the confusion and frustration and foggy cloud which had been over my brain to one degree or another since I'd been told of Lynn's death.

Barbara's voice indicated that she seemed to sense the same thing that I did about this; that we wouldn't be seeing each other until this was all behind me.

"Be careful. And...and..." She rushed up to me, her arms going under mine, from behind. She held herself close for a moment. "I...I...just don't get hurt...oh, please take care of yourself! I want you in one piece!"

Then, without another word, she flashed past me. For one brief moment I had a full view of her face. Her large lovely eyes. Her full, red lips. It seemed that her eyes were moist, and her lips trembling. But I wasn't sure. And the fact left my awareness a second after I recorded it. The whirl of other thoughts, more demanding, important, urgent, clouded over every other idea and emotional response.

This time I wouldn't stop until I began to see the finish. I wouldn't stop until I had that creepy bastard between my fingers, squeezing the life out of him.

Whoever it was—was dead! There was a living dead man, right at this moment. Somewhere in the city he was walking and breathing his last moments of life. And his hunter and killer was now, full-time, on his trail.

☛Chapter Nine☚

I sat outside in my car for a long time, just thinking. One thing was for certain. I had to face the fact that I'd have to see Theresa DeBray again. The first meeting had been cut far too short to really get any help from her. Another fact about the DeBray woman was that she knew a lot of things that she hadn't told me. She had actually done more to confuse the situation than help it. A few answers had been given but they created more questions.

For every answer I seemed to get two or three new questions, making the puzzle get more complex.

Another thing to consider was that the police were also working on finding the rape artist. They had more information than I did. They had a better start. They had a larger and better-trained force working to get the same information that I was trying to get. And they weren't wasting any time. And I was a prime suspect for murder, too.

But there were some factors in my favor. If necessary, I could get rough. It was possible for me to beat information out of a person where the police couldn't get away with such brutal tactics.

That might get me in trouble, later, but I just didn't give a damn!

And another point was that while some people might not be willing to talk to the law, they *would* talk to a private party. On the other hand, there were those who would do just the opposite. It all depended on who had the facts; the ones who would talk to me or the ones who would blab to the police.

Still, there was the third group of people. Those who wouldn't talk to anybody because they were protecting someone, either themselves or friends or relatives. That thought hit me for the first time. Maybe because I was thinking more clearly now.

The DeBray woman had been looking for something in Lynn's apartment. The question was: What and why?

The "what" part I couldn't answer, but the "why" I might be able to. Maybe she had a boy friend or brother who was connected with Lynn. Someone she was afraid the police would find out about. Was she protecting somebody?

And what about the murdered man, Derk Meechan? What connection did he have with Lynn? Or DeBray?

Could he be the man driving the car for her when she got away from me the evening before?

It might have helped if I'd been a mystery fan. But when it came to solving mysteries of any kind I was a complete amateur. And that helped a lot. I had to play things by ear. And by ear they sounded as confusing as hell. All flat tones, no sharps. Just a lot of minors and discordant sounds.

One fact kept hammering home. I'd have to see the woman again. And that was one meeting I wasn't really looking forward to. She was an enigma that I didn't wish to be forced to face. It was like having to stand by, while a group of the most beautiful women in the world stripped themselves naked as they proceeded to do everything possible to excite my hormones to moan with hot desire, while I was strapped down to the floor helpless to resist. I couldn't move. They wouldn't do anything more than tease me with their wanton displays. It was the kind of torturous hell that no man wished to subject himself to. Maybe roughly exciting—but still hellish!

But there didn't seem to be any better place or way to begin. She had the answers to a lot of questions, which I needed, before I could do anything else.

Sighing heavily, I tiredly started the car and headed it in the direction of her home. It seemed as if I'd been going around in circles all day. Around in circles, chasing my tail! Wasting time and energy.

But a few hours with Barbara had actually helped to clear away some of the cobs webbing my brain.

Twenty minutes later I arrived at the DeBray home.

78

The lights were on and I parked the car, got out and walked across that long stretch of lawn.

Then I was ringing the doorbell.

I expected Ben, the butler. I was in for a surprise because a young man in his middle twenties answered the door. He was obviously drunk. That was the first thing I noticed about him.

His black hair was one series of curling locks after another. He wore a formal dinner jacket that was pressed perfectly; and maybe a couple of hours before it had been neat but now it had several other creases in it. He took one quick look at me and smiled broadly.

"Well, sir, what can I do for you?" he asked, bowing grandly, almost spilling the drink in his hand.

"Is Mrs. DeBray in?"

He sobered slightly at the sound of her name. "Who the hell are you?"

"Stan Matson."

His smile beamed once more. "Well now, Stanley boy, just the man I've been wanting to see. Yes, sir! Just the man! Come on in. Come on in!"

I was slightly stunned by his seeming anxiousness to see me. A little puzzled. The door closed behind us. He laid an arm on my shoulder. It felt like a lead weight. "Well, buddy, old pal. How about a drink?"

"No, I don't think so..."

"Come on! Don't be a dull man. There's plenty of it. Endless stream of golden liquid of every kind. Why be shy? I'm not. Never was!"

He was walking across the room toward the study where I'd seen Theresa DeBray that afternoon. I followed, still slightly dazed, and maybe expecting to find the mistress of the house there. She wasn't.

"Where's Mrs. DeBray?"

He ignored the question. Instead, he was walking over to the cabinet. After a moment of silence, while he mixed the drink that I didn't want, he turned and walked back across the room to the entrance where I stood.

"Here!" he announced, handing me the drink. I took it. "Bottoms up! Live while you can. You never know what tomorrow might not bring."

I jolted. Tried to remember where I'd heard that same expression before. Then it came to me. Linda Clifford.

"You know Linda Clifford?" I asked guardedly. Casually I sipped a little of the drink.

"That wild tramp? Sure thing!" He smiled again, and then placed that heavy arm on me again. "A regular member of the club, already?" He laughed, pushing me forward into the room. "You know, I like you already. Sure do."

It was amazing. There wasn't any doubt that he was loaded all the way up, yet his actions were steady enough and his words un-slurred. He took a strong gulp of his drink. From the color it looked like straight liquor.

"Where's Mrs. DeBray?"

"Oh, come on, buddy. Don't go acting formal with me. After what I heard about you this afternoon... I think you can call her Theresa. Everybody calls her that, anybody who *really* knows her." The gleam in his eye seemed to be implying much – which made me feel somewhat uncomfortable.

"Nothing happened," I told him, feeling uneasy.

"Nothing *happened?*" He laughed and moved away, turning and studying me with a strange light in his eyes. "From what Theresa told me, you charged all her burners and she's ready, willing and anxious to take your rocket into endless space with her."

I didn't wish to continue along that line of conversation. In fact, I was beginning to wonder what I was doing in here, talking to a total stranger. "Mind telling me who you are?"

"Sure, buddy. Just call me Eddy. Eddy DeBray. Theresa married my old man!"

For a moment I thought that one over. *A new piece in the puzzle?* I didn't have any way of knowing at that point. But maybe this was a bit of luck. Finding him in the condition he was in. Maybe if I drank along with him he'd really open up and give information about the people I was most interested in hearing about.

If he knew Linda Clifford, then he knew Lynn.

I asked him about Lynn.

"Oh, that little slut. Well, okay, hot slut, if you must.

80

One of the best sluts around, come to think of it."

I tensed at the phrase but I kept from reacting violently. If he were baiting me on purpose it wouldn't be to my advantage to bite. I wanted information; and whatever he might have to say about Lynn would be a great help to me—nicely put or not.

"A real hot body in bed. And what a party giver..." *He* broke off, suddenly. His face became abruptly red and his eyes looked into his glass. "Hell, I'm sorry. I forgot. You're her brother."

There was an awkward silence after that.

"Go on anyway. I want to know about Lynn," I finally encouraged.

"Well, there's...well, nothing much to say. She was just a member of the gang that Theresa ran around with before she met Dad. I brought her around once to meet the old man and that was the end of little old Eddy-boy." His hands were clamping around the glass, squeezing violently. His voice bitter. "The only thing was, after they got married, Eddy-boy was there after-hours to fill in for what the old man who didn't have all the juice to please his hot young bride." He grinned savagely. "Old fella used to be famous in special circles as quite a stud. But, well, even the best get tamed with age. And dear, hot, lovin', wild Theresa didn't stop with me. There were other boyfriends, which she carried on with, on the side. A high-class looking little tramp." He shrugged. "But then the whole gang was that way."

I gulped at the glass in my hands. What I was hearing and what it meant about Lynn was causing a hard knot of agony to tie up inside me. I needed to loosen it a bit.

"About Lynn, though," Eddy continued, brightening slightly. "She was a little different, in a way."

My heart seemed to pause. Then it got sicker when he continued.

"High Queen of the society of Sex for Sex sake!" he laughed and took another swallow from his glass, draining it. Then he walked over to the bar-cabinet, poured himself another drink, downed some of it and then turned toward me. "You might say that she started the whole thing. Most of the original group consisted of friends she ran around with. Like

81

Theresa and myself and a couple others. That group attracted more people, like Linda and Derk."

"Derk? Derk Meechan?"

"Yeah. Who else? That dirty son-of-a-bitch had all the women clawing to climb into bed with him. They couldn't grab at him enough! He was using Lynn and Theresa against each other. Playing racket ball with their boobies, so to speak. And they played tennis with his...tennis balls!"

He stood there for a long time in silence. His hand was holding onto the bookcase, gripping the wood for support. The tight fury in his face was a twisted insane anger. Red and distorted. Then he relaxed. "But between Derk and Lynn, we had some real dedicated swingers.

"Like the New Year's party. Had to come naked at that one. The games were wild!" He laughed loudly, doubling over and slapping his leg. "You should have been there. From what Lynn told us of you, I could never understand why you didn't run around with our crowd. You sounded like you'd have been High Priest!"

"We didn't see eye-to-eye about certain matters," I explained, hoping to sidetrack the conversation so that I wouldn't have to hear any more about her wild parties. For the first time I was beginning to look at life a little differently. Up to then everything had been wine, women and song. No thought of settling down. Just have one blast-out after another. Hearing about Lynn's activities was making me suddenly look at my own in a different light. Where would it end? I could see several endings. I'd seen some of them. Linda Clifford ran so wild that she would dope a total stranger to get things rolling. Then there was Theresa DeBray. What had her life ended up as? Legalized whore for big money, at the same time giving herself to her husband's son and any other man who might come along. At least I read it that way.

And then there was Lynn. Raped and killed.

Where would it all end? My own life?

I'd never thought of it all in that way before. And right then I didn't have time to think about it long.

Looking up at Eddy DeBray again, I asked: "What

about what happened to Lynn? You have any idea how that might have happened?"

That insane red fury returned to his features. "That little cheap tease..." Then his voice calmed a little and he shook his head. "Actually—well, your little sister was quite a combination. Rack up or shut up. She also got kicks out of driving a man to the point of no return and then denying him the object of his desires—her body." He shrugged once more. "Still, you'd think that the guy who did that thing to her would have...well, she would have given in...*what I mean,*" he quickly explained, "is that you'd think she'd have given in before...the man killed her."

I couldn't agree or disagree. I didn't know enough about Lynn. So many cross impressions. Too many faces. Sex-lover. Tease. Little sister. It all still seemed a little fantastic to realize what kind of person she must have been.

Just then the double doors flung open and in rushed Theresa DeBray. Dressed much like I'd seen her the first time. All High Class Fashion model but with a more voluptuous figure.

From the expression on her face I could see she was both mad and... something else. That emotion I couldn't figure out.

"What has he been telling you?" she asked me in an evenly controlled voice. "I imagine a lot of lies. A lot of damn lies!" She turned on Eddy. "You're just a no-good goddamned drunken bum!" Her voice wasn't controlled any more. It was high-pitched and screaming. *"Get the hell out of this room!"*

He looked at her for a long moment; that insane fury that he'd shown several times, while I had been talking to him, clouded his features. Then he laughed. Picked up a bottle from the bar-cabinet and started across the room. Theresa stepped in front of him.

"Give me that bottle!" she snapped, slapping him across the face. "Give it to me, you little creep!"

His expression whitened. The bottle dropped to the floor, the glass in his other hand followed it. His fists doubled up, one arm starting to swing back. Then he glanced at me. He turned, smiled and then looked once more at Theresa.

His words came out softly between tightly clenched teeth. I could hardly make them out.

"You little whore. One of these days I'll kill you... you'll be dead just like..." his eyes moved in my direction for just a second, then he continued, "just like *that!*"

"Eddy!" Theresa screamed over his words.

They froze. Each staring furiously at the other. Then Eddy moved around Theresa and walked out of the room, slamming the doors loudly behind him.

☛Chapter Ten☚

For a long time the two of us stood in silence not looking at each other. I was slightly embarrassed and quite a bit confused. I didn't know whether to be mad at Eddy or Theresa. Right then I felt like striking out at each of them.

"Well, that was that," she sighed, turning and looking at me full in the face. Her mouth smiled. "What can I do for you this time?"

I shrugged. For a moment I didn't know what to say. Still swallowing the scene with my startled eyes. The sudden, unaccounted for blowup had left me a little numb.

"I guess you're wondering about that... little performance?" Her voice was strangely pleasant. She acted as if she were actually glad to see me.

I shrugged again. "None of my business, I guess."

She didn't say anything. Instead, she moved over to the bar-cabinet, picked out a glass for herself and, after placing ice in it, filled it with straight whiskey. The smashed bottle and whiskey glass lay scattered and untouched in the middle of the floor. She didn't even seem to notice it or care about it.

"Want a drink?" she offered.

"Have one." After arching an eyebrow and taking a sip of the whiskey, she stepped over to a chair and sat down. "Now, what can I do for you?"

"A little information."

"You're acting like a private dick... or something. Is that was you are? A private...dick?"

That last she made sound bluntly suggestive.

"Or something. I want to find out about..."

"Lynn! Don't tell me. Let me guess. Lynn, Lynn,

Lynn, always dear, hot, little Lynn!"

"Can we start where we left off this afternoon?"

"What are you really after, Mr. Matson? Why not let the police handle this affair? Really none of our business, don't you think?"

"I think it's my business." I took a swallow of the drink. It was like water; it didn't do a thing for me. Only moistened my dry throat.

She rearranged herself in the chair. The action had a sexual quality about it that reminded me of that electric shock we'd shared. "You shouldn't try to do police business. Didn't your mommy tell you that? Or was it your daddy? I forgot. Never mind. The authorities are far better at it than you could ever be."

Her hand was resting on her thigh, the fingers curving inwards. They moved idly. "And, anyway, aren't there other things, more interesting, to do besides trying to run down...?"

"Look! I'm serious about it."

"I don't see what you can do that the police can't do better!" she snapped back. "Anyway. They aren't even getting hot! They're cold as..." She caught herself, abruptly aware that she'd been speaking out loud.

"What do you mean, they're cold?" I asked, stepping anxiously forward.

She looked up at me, her eyes frightened looking for a moment. Then they seemed to take on a glow of sensual mystery, as if she had willfully drawn an invisible screen across her mind. "Oh, it's just a...well, guess! You know Lynn. Oh, but then, you don't, do you? You never *did* understand her, did you? Still, that doesn't matter. Now. Yet, if you had known her, you'd realize what I meant about the police being cold."

She stood then and started to move toward me. "But why talk of such morbid things?"

"That's why I came here."

She laughed. It was a throaty sound that moved the silky white texture of her smooth throat. "Oh, come on! You can't fool Theresa. After what happened this afternoon." She was almost to me, and both her arms reached outwards. Be-

86

fore I could stop her or protest, her arms were around my neck. Then she moved in very close. I felt the hard, demanding pressure as her hips circled in against mine, then they surged up violently. She wasn't making any attempt to be subtle in any possible way. Blunt was her totality.

"Come on, you can't fool Theresa," she murmured in a low sensual voice, "that touch, this morning. Oh, how delicious. We both felt it. Didn't we? The wonderful electric thrill, that's what you came for! Now, baby, tell me the truth. Don't you want to just drown in that electric pleasure – the hot yielding fire of my body?"

I was helpless. The first contact had sent my head spinning. My heart was throbbing in my throat. Everything inside me was racing madly. The electric thrill, as she called it, was rushing through every cell like an overwhelming shock. It was stunning. All I could do was stand there, paralyzed by the white heat and pulsing desire that was building like an insanely speeding rocket, going into orbit.

Her cheek caressed mine and then her lips gently touched my mouth and all hell started to spin loose.

There would be something wrong with me if I didn't admit that I found, at that moment, it almost impossible not to give in to Theresa. And, as much as I have always hated those scenes in movies when a woman does such things to a man and the guy turns her down, I now realized why they could do just that.

I had to fight every crying nerve in my body to keep from responding directly to her raw overture.

Forcefully, I set my hands on her shoulders. For a moment she misunderstood what I was trying to do. A contented sigh pushed up through her lips and she squeezed herself tighter to me. With all the effort I had, physically, mentally and emotionally, I pushed her away. It was like trying to peel an outer layer of skin off. She clung rigidly and frantically.

"Damn it all!" I muttered between clenched teeth. "No!"

I held her out at arm's length. She was just about the most delightfully wild sight I'd ever seen. Somehow her hair had become tangled and undone during the quick struggle.

Her dress had managed to become loosened off one shoulder and a half-covered breast was attractively revealed. Her cream-white skin was lovely beyond my ability to describe. It might have been the fact that I was refusing this offering that made it seem the most desirable bed-tumble I'd ever had the chance to have.

She frowned as if she couldn't believe that I was refusing her.

"Don't you like women?" she asked in a thin, tight voice. "Or is it just me?"

"That has nothing to do with it!"

"I think it does. No man would turn...no man has *ever* turned me down cold, like that!" She seemed more curious than mad or hurt.

"How can you do it?" That question held a lot of admiration and a little contempt.

I didn't have any answer to that. It seemed like she couldn't understand that, sometimes, there are more important things than sex; or, that a man likes to choose and decide such matters for himself.

"Let's put it this way. I was telling the truth when I said I wanted to find the man who killed Lynn."

"I don't believe it!" She was walking back to her chair. "I just don't believe it!" Her voice was at a height of disbelief. "Crap. I can't believe it!"

"What was this all about. You and Eddy?"

She shot a look at me and then her eyes returned to the glass in her hands.

"Well?"

"A family matter." The words were low and hard to hear.

"He said you both knew Derk."

"I told you he was a liar!"

"He mentioned him first!"

Once more her eyes jerked to mine, only to drop again.

"What about him?"

"I don't see why I have to answer questions!" she snapped, anger forehead.

"Because I think you know something..."

88

"I know a lot of things..." She smiled this time. It was one of those expressions a woman will throw at a man when she's trying to make him wonder just what those *other* things might be. The implication was sexual. She seemed to be running on one track. Or maybe she thought that was the best way to divert a man's attention.

"Stop avoiding the issue..."

"I'll do exactly what I damn please in my house!"

She stood. Then smiled once more. "But why don't you just forget all about this? It's not going to get you anywhere. And we could be having so much fun together. Why not be a sport?"

"Sit down!"

"Go to hell!" Her lips smiled as she said the words.

I was prepared for her next move yet I couldn't stop her.

She pulled down the top of her dress. "Why don't you come on over here? Give these a feel! Most men can't get enough of kissing and touching them. Now, honey, be honest...please.... Wouldn't you like to just smother against them?"

A hard knot lumped in my throat. I was latterly sweating.

Before I could move she dropped the dress down farther. "Come on, big boy! Let's see what makes *you* tick! Tick tick tick! Tick tock. Ring my clock! But you have a ringer that dings and dongs a girl like wild!"

It was like being strapped down and unable to move. I watched, fascinated. Who wouldn't be? She was a lovely woman. Tall and regal. Full and beautiful. Every curve was brimming over with supple looking flesh. It was far too attractive to stop looking at. She knew exactly what she was doing, and how to make it irresistible. Her body was so damned delicious to look at and had to be even more heavenly to just submerge into that I was paralyzed.

"Come on, honey!" she cooed. "I'm so good I'll send you to heaven and back like you've never been sent. Oh, come to me, baby."

I didn't even have time to realize what she was doing, before she leaped across the space between us. Her arms flung around my neck.

Electric charging fury flooded between us; overpowering me. It took control of my body, for the moment, leaving my mind helpless to do anything but look on, slightly aghast.

I felt her hands rush over me, my pants being opened as the feel of her searching fingers came trembling against my flesh.

"Oh, *big* daddy!" she moaned in delight, literally ripping at my clothing in her desperate desire to possess me. "Oh, by God!

She moaned, literally shivering in utter delight. Electric fires seemed to drag through my own body so overpowering that I couldn't stop my own hands from grabbing at her, greedily gathering the woman into my grip. We just stood there for a long, lingering moment, aware of what was about to happen, challenging the other to make the first move.

She moaned again, coming up closer. "Deliver us to Heaven, oh Lordy, mine!"

☛Chapter Eleven☚

Some time later I was sitting bewilderedly in a small bar, a jukebox playing some noisy rock and roll arrangement. I hardly noticed. The drink in my hand was already half finished. It was the third highball. Nothing seemed to help. All I could think about was what had happened between me and Teresa DeBray. The feel of her. The taste of her. The utter overpowering seduction of that unyielding, wonderful body.

Then something had snapped inside me. The rigid wall of resistance that my mind had been trying to break through finally disintegrated into nothingness. And only disgusted contempt was left to replace the searing, white heat that had all but taken complete control over my body.

Roughly, I had clawed her away from me with a violent push. She stood, like a gigantic goddess, staring at me. Then backed away.

"Screw you!" she snarled, as I turned to leave.

But the insane laughter followed me out of the room, and the taunting challenge that she screeched after that, caused my stomach to wrench. The woman didn't even really seem to care. It was all an ugly game to her.

"I'll get you! We haven't even started! You'll beg for my body!" Her almost insane laugh followed me out of that house.

In the bar I was feeling mixed emotions and mental reactions to what strange encounter.

There was the normal regret, which any man would feel. She was more than just a sexy female. She was sex itself. Naturally, my body wished that I had taken her offer and consumed the fires of hell with her. That was simply a physical craving. Emotionally, I didn't really give a bloody damn. Mentally, it made me sick.

I sensed an illness running through all the people that I'd come in contact with who had been part of Lynn's world. They seemed to be plagued with an abnormally cancerous sex drive. They didn't seem to have any idea what it meant to be interested in other things. Nor did they know the same limits that most normal people seem to understand.

I'd thought that Barbara had been bad, before I came in contact with Linda Clifford. Linda Clifford had seemed pretty wild. At least she had enough sense to take 'no' for answer in a rather ribald way. Theresa DeBray didn't seem to have even that much sanity. She just laughed when I turned her down for the second time in a row within minutes. She laughed and challenged. It was even more frightening.

Suddenly I wanted to talk to Barbara. But I held back the impulse to go to the phone and call her. It was odd how a person could change their viewpoint.

Barbara seemed to be taking on a new meaning in my eyes. The woman seemed to be evolving into an island of lovely caring and a safe place to be surrounded in soft understanding. Everything in me simply wanted to be enveloped in her arms almost like a child being comforted by its mother. Not that she was a mothering type. I mean, you could hardly get that close to Barbara without feeling other surging desires. But sex was the furthest thing on my mind. I simply wanted to be with somebody who was sane and cared about me as a human being.

I took another strong swallow of the drink, downing the rest of the contents. Motioning the barman over, I ordered another. "This time just the straight stuff—no chaser!"

For the first time since I'd started, I was up against a blank wall and I knew it.

I couldn't face Theresa any more. She was determined to get only one thing from our relationship. That was the one thing I wanted to avoid. I wanted answers. She wasn't willing to give them.

Then a thought struck me. She had always managed to sidetrack the questions when they started to get down to real cases. First, threatening to call the police. Then saying that what I was doing was a waste of time.

Then by making a direct pass. Then another more naked and brazen assault.

If it weren't for my male ego, supported by several facts, I'd find it quite easy to believe that she had used her sex and body to just sidetrack the questioning. To avoid. What an avoidance, too!

The facts were: the electric quality of our touch; the statement that Eddy DeBray had made about her wanting to get at me; and most importantly, she could have called the police and had me ordered out of the house by law. And thrown into jail. That was obvious.

What kind of game was Theresa playing?

Also, the truth about her own, apparent, sexual desires was another issue. She seemed to lust for every man she could get to take her body.

But she had also been using that body to keep from answering my questions. She had gone out of her way not to give honest answers to the ones she *had* responded to. Saying that Eddy was a liar. I began thinking that maybe he was telling the truth. Maybe the information I wanted would be just as easy to get from him. In fact, a lot easier. There wasn't the sexual complication between us. And he seemed willing enough to talk in detail.

He was a new factor in the case. He knew Lynn. He also ran around in the same group. He knew Derk Meechan. And there was that... The psychotic way he acted. One moment laughing, the next, mad to the point of insanity.

I was running into a series of odd and psychotic people. Two women and one man. All three having some direct connection to Lynn. What kind of person had my kid sister become?

And why did Theresa deny knowing Meechan?

The pieces were falling together in some shadowy form. In fact, too shadowy and dark. I wasn't sure exactly what the shape was or what it might mean, if I could see it. But suddenly I was aware that most of the facts were there. Like you buy a picture puzzle. All the pieces are there and you lose the "key" picture so the only way you will ever discover the subject matter is to put the puzzle together the hard way. Piece by piece. Not force them; just slowly, carefully discover which ones fit, which one's didn't, move them around and try again and again.

The only thing was, I didn't know where to start.

Of course there was the logical way to begin. Start from the center and work outwards. The trouble was: where did I look to find the center?

Lynn's death.

That might be a focal point.

The major pieces circulating around that fact were: Linda Clifford, Theresa DeBray,

Eddy, Derk Meechan, and the rape artist.

Meechan wasn't the rapist—at least the police didn't seem to think so or they would have held me for the murder.

Eddy was the only other man.

It hardly seemed logical that Eddy would have. No doubt, Lynn and he had already had a few tumbles and he was more than casually interested in Theresa.

Mr. X.

I didn't think that I'd found him, yet. Maybe that was the missing picture.

Mr. X might have been somebody who didn't know Lynn. Otherwise, why would he have raped her? From what I'd discovered about my sister I could pretty well guess that there wouldn't have been any struggle.

Then a thought suggested itself to me.

What if Lynn had been murdered and then the person who did it made it look like it was merely a rape?

I quickly rejected the idea. Not that it wasn't possible; only that I couldn't see any possible reason for anybody having done such a thing.

So far I had three people who might give me answers. Eddy, Theresa and Linda. The two women were basic problems—for obvious reasons. Eddy DeBray might have a few more answers. The only thing was that I'd have to get to him without Theresa being around.

But, what if Lynn had been murdered by someone and then the person made it look like rape?

That thought hammered back at me, again...and then...I thought.

Could a woman have killed Lynn and then made it

94

look like rape?

That was impossible. 1 didn't know, for sure; not being a doctor. But hardly reasonable. Not even sane.

More likely some stranger had come along, seen her lush body and figured it was ripe for the picking.

But rape wasn't about sex. Was it? Power was the name of the game.

Some bastard creep had seen Lynn, decided she was a likely target for his rage and simply grabbed her and did his filthy little savage job on her soft young body.

Or somebody she worked for who might not have enjoyed a tumble with this lovely female so famous for being a hot slut.

My mind screamed in panic: *Oh, God, what's wrong with me?*

I was desperately clinging to any fantasy possible. I was struggling with half-assed images, theories, and make-believe in a frantic need to create sense out of what didn't make any sense at all.

My head was reeling as if attacked by a storm. A frantic wind of thoughts were hammering together, blurring and becoming shapeless. My mind was spinning around in that torrent of confusion, unable to make any sense out of it.

1 gulped down the shot of whiskey and ordered another. When it came, I quickly let it follow the course of the first one.

Suddenly, I was beginning to wonder if, maybe, I had bitten off more than I could handle. That maybe I was beaten before starting.

The drinks were making me slightly lightheaded now. Abruptly I wanted to sleep. I was tired. I needed some rest. Not so much from physical tiredness, but mental fatigue. Too many ideas whirling around for my overworked brain to sort out.

Rest was the most important thing, right now. I walked out of the bar to where my car was parked down the street.

The drive back to the apartment was a long, weary job. But I finally made it. Several times I was afraid I'd weave off the road, but managed to keep in a straight line.

The wonder was that some cop didn't stop me. Luck was with me on this side of the scale; but if I had been caught I'd have avoided what was about to take place the moment I entered my rooms.

The lights were out. I was just reaching for the switch when the darkness became painful reality; a black explosive pain jolted through my body, starting at the base of my skull where some hammer-like object made contact.

The world whipped around, then the floor smashed up into my face.

The next thing that ebbed through my awareness was the throbbing of a pinpoint of light, high above me. It was out of focus. A hundred miles out in space. Then, slowly, it started getting bigger and bigger. It was speeding down toward me. I struggled to escape it. For some reason it seemed as if I was in some kind of danger. Then abruptly it opened up into a full, three-dimensional world of reality.

I was lying on my back in the middle of my living room.

My first reaction was; *one more factor to add.*

Why? Who?

Painfully, I stood and looked around me. My head was throbbing with a living pulse all its own. When I saw my surroundings the beat became more painful, faster.

The room was turned upside down. Somebody had been looking for something when I'd turned up. Whoever it was had been in a hurry and not taken the time to be neat or orderly. It looked like a pack of wild monkeys had been set loose in my apartment. Everything had been touched, one way or another.

The second reaction was; *the dirty bastard who did this would pay through the teeth! So help me God!*

There wasn't any time to think things out. The phone rang. I walked over to the stand where it lay almost upturned. I picked up the receiver. "Hello?"

"Stanny-boy!" Barbara's voice cried happily. Just what I needed right then—a social talk with a woman I wanted to be with more than anything else.

"Can I call you later?"

"Anything wrong?"

96

"Let's say a storm hit my room!"

"What?"

"Somebody was here last night and decided to rearrange my room!"

"Who?"

"That's a Class A question."

"Why would anybody do that?"

"Another good question."

"Anything I can do?"

"I don't think so."

"Help clean up?"

"...I don't know. Right now my head feels like it's been put through a meat-grinder. Somebody used it for a batting ball last night. One strike and I was out! I must have caught them in the act and they didn't want to let me in on the action."

"Oh, no! You poor thing. I'll be right over."

The phone clicked and I realized she'd hung up. I slowly replaced the receiver.

I was on my way across the room toward the kitchen for a glass of water when the phone rang again. It had given two rings when I had the receiver in my hand once more. "Look, Barbara... "

The man's voice on the other end cut me short. "This Mr. Matson?"

I shook my head, feeling like a damned fool, not quite sure what to say.

"Yeah who's this?" I finally answered.

"Police Lieutenant Johnson wants to see you"

That was a switch. Instead of an escort he was requesting my presence. Maybe things were looking up between the law and me.

"What for?" I asked, "This time. No escort?"

"He said to just tell you to come down to the station as soon as you could."

"Okay. I have a few things to take care of, first."

"Better make it snappy. The lieutenant doesn't like to be kept waiting."

For a moment I had the impulse to say something snappy back but then decided there was no point in going out of my way to antagonize the police department, especially Lt. Johnson. Anyway, there were a few things I wanted to talk to him about. Maybe I could get a little information from him.

Then the thought hit me:

Had the police tabbed the rape artist?

I didn't dare ask the question.

"Okay," I told the man on the other end of the phone. "I'll be right over."

After hanging up and fixing myself a glass of cold water, following it with a short shot of whiskey, I changed my clothes and carefully examined the place where my head had made contact with a solid object the night before. There was a small tight lump there.

Then, after writing a note to Barbara, I walked out of the apartment and down the steps, outside and into my car.

Then the police station.

The walk up to Lt. Johnson's office was short. He was quick to greet me. His face grim. His words directly to the point.

"What do you know about Theresa DeBray?"

I gulped, more from surprise than anything. Up to this time he had made it a point *not* to mention the woman's name. Now he was coming right out with it.

"What do you mean?"

"Exactly what do you know about her?"

"What do *you* know about her?" I countered, stalling for time and trying to organize my thoughts to this new twist.

What did the police want to know about her?

And why were they asking *me?*

"Just answer the questions!" Johnson demanded, walking around to the other side of his desk and sitting down.

"I don't get it!" Slowly I took out a cigarette and, taking my time, lighted up. One thing that I wanted to do was find out exactly what the questioning was for, before I put my foot into it—like I'd done the morning before "Just what's the bit? You aren't interested in her for social reasons. And what could I tell you that you don't know already about her?"

98

"Maybe a lot." He sighed heavily and then, after looking at me for a long careful moment, he took a deep breath. "I might as well level with you.

"Theresa DeBray was found dead last night. And you're the one person who might be able to give us a lead on the matter."

MURDER TIMES FOUR, BY CHARLES NUETZEL

☙Chapter Twelve☙

I sat there for a long time trying to wade through the thick cloud of surprise and shock. It seemed impossible that she could be dead. And for what reason? I shook my head and looked across at the lieutenant. "Who?"

"What?"

"Who did it?"

"We don't know. That's why I asked you to come down."

"You don't think that I..."

"No, you didn't do it. We've had a man on you ever since you left here yesterday morning."

That was another blow.

"Thanks for nothing!" I grumbled, taking a nervous drag from the cigarette.

"You should be glad. Otherwise we'd have picked you up. But there is one thing that we do know. Theresa was alive when you left her last night."

"How do you know?"

"One of my men went to her for questioning. She was also a possible suspect on this Meechan case. Now we think maybe it might have been Eddy DeBray—that would be..."

"Yeah, I met him."

"Well, we can't find him anyplace. He's disappeared."

My mind was beginning to tick with a more intelligent degree of effectiveness. I was beginning to find it possible to add a couple of pieces together and start seeing what the picture might look like.

What if Eddy DeBray had been the rape artist? What if he had killed Theresa because she had known about it?

What if he had been the person in my apartment the night before? What if he had killed Derk Meechan?

But I couldn't get an answer to satisfy all those questions.

Eddy might have been the rape artist. But why? He knew Lynn. And what was it he had called her, before he stopped himself? *A slut!* The tone of voice he had used was cold contempt. And why? Then, later he had, once more, stopped himself when he said; *That little cheap tease.*

He'd called Derk Meechan a dirty bastard. Violence was in his voice then. But still, I couldn't see any real motive. Maybe because I didn't have all the facts.

"What about the murderer of my sister? Have you found out anything about it?"

The lieutenant did a double take. "You kidding?"

"No. Why?"

"Whoever raped and killed your sister, raped and killed Mrs. DeBray."

"And you think that it might be Eddy DeBray?" I asked, guardedly controlling my voice to show no emotion.

"We don't know. He ran around with her before she met his father. That much we have found out."

That meant that they had found out a lot of what I had discovered. "What's the point of questioning me?"

"Simple." He paused, looked briefly at me and then at his desk. "You might think our police force can get all the information it wants. That's not always the truth. Not in this case, anyway! There are several reasons for us to believe you were able to find out things that our men didn't get a chance to discover. That's why we let you free so quickly..."

"Thanks loads!"

"No, don't get us wrong. We didn't have anything on you, but by letting you take off and putting a man on you, we hoped to maybe find out a few things. We did find out that the trail led to the DeBrays."

"Which meant?"

"That we had every reason to believe that they are, in some way, connected with your sister's death. Why was Mrs. DeBray at your sister's apartment?"

"Then you believed my story."

"Of course we did. You were an eyewitness able not only to produce the gun, registered under Mrs. DeBray's husband's name but the car license matched. There wasn't any doubt about that..."

"Then..."

"So then we had a man put on your trail. And it ended at the DeBrays'. You landed there twice. Gave our man quite a running around..."

"Nothing surprising about that," I sighed, getting nervous about talking about Theresa DeBray. "She was a lovely woman, and didn't seem to mind showing off her more attractive features. To put it bluntly: she was a bit..."

"Over-sexed?" the lieutenant finished, standing and moving around to my side of the desk once more.

"Yeah, you might put it that way."

He laughed. "She tried putting on an act for me."

I could imagine.

"But this is getting beside the point." He leaned closer to me. "Did you find out anything which might help us?"

I thought that over. How much *had* I actually found out? That was one thing that was hard to add up—because it didn't amount to anything that I could put my finger on. And on the other hand, did I want to tell what little I *did* know?

"Well?"

"Hardly anything to tell you. The trail ended with Theresa DeBray. I was looking for her. She was the only lead I had. You haven't even told me where Lynn was killed."

He nodded silently at that.

"And even if I did have information, what makes you think I'd give it to you?"

He just looked at me.

"After all, from your point of view, I'm out to get and kill the man who..."

"Drop the act!" The man moved back of his desk again. "So you aren't going to tell us anything."

"I didn't say that." I took a careful drag on the cigarette. "All I'm telling you is that from my point of view there's hardly any reason to be handing out information..."

103

"Ever heard of just helping the law?" he asked sarcastically.

"Don't think that it applies here!"

"Applies? Damn it all, man, don't you realize that we are working *for* you—not against you? Our job is to keep things orderly for society! We're here to serve, not do disservice to the public. Too many of you people think we're just here to give out traffic tickets, bug and bother you. Kids are growing up with the idea that the police force is against them, rather for them. They don't stop to consider that we're dedicated to control violence, not give it out! They scream about police brutality and forget that some people—even us—don't find it very enjoyable being shot at, pushed around, called names, misunderstood. We're guys doing a job—just a job trying to help people like you! So just get off your blasted high-horse. If somebody gets hurt or killed, then it is up to us to see to it that they get put away—"

"That's just it. The man who did that to my sister doesn't deserve to just be put away!"

"You can't put yourself above a judge and jury. Above the rules of society!"

Both of us had been shouting and now we paused for breath. The outburst had come unexpectedly and both of us were slightly out of breath. Perhaps each of us was under the same frustrated pressure cooker yielding no answers to a horrid puzzle which just seemed to get worse from dead body to dead body.

Finally I said, "Look, to be truthful, I just don't know anything. I've run up against a blind alley. Last night I'd all but given in; returned home, when somebody whacked me over the head."

"What?" Johnson stiffened with surprise. "Why?"

"You think I'd be here if I knew?"

Silence answered me. Then finally he said tiredly. "You may go."

"What the hell does that mean?"

"You may go. I've found out all *I* wanted to know."

"What?" It was my turn to be shocked.

"Exactly what I said. You say you don't know anything, so let's leave it at that!"

I turned to leave and his voice stopped me for a moment. "I'd be careful, if I were you."

I turned. "What does that mean?"

"Just be careful."

I wasn't sure if he were threatening or just giving me a friendly piece of advice.

Once outside and sitting behind the wheel, driving along the freeway, I had time to think about what had gone on in the lieutenant's office. It didn't make sense. A few quick questions, with no answers and then he abruptly cut the conversation short.

One thing seemed to be hammering in the back of my head.

Lt. Johnson wasn't a fool. He obviously had something going for him and he wasn't letting me in on it.

What, I didn't know. But it had to do with something that I had said.

I'd told him about my being hit on the head and then he had dropped the whole interview.

No further questions.

Why hadn't I told him more? Actually there was more reason to help the police department than fight them. They were, as they had pointed out, on my side. Yet, for some reason, I had refused to tell him anything.

Still, what was there to tell? Nothing. Just that I'd met Eddy DeBray and that he was slightly unbalanced. That I'd met and been royally seduced by Linda Clifford. That Derk Meechan, Linda, Eddy and Theresa had run around with Lynn.

It didn't mean anything – yet. Nothing added up to any solution. It was just a series of facts with seemingly no real connection to the rape and killing of Lynn Matson. There were the facts. They kept rattling around. Shifting and re-shifting, getting no place. Even the police were puzzled by what they couldn't find out. They thought Eddy DeBray might have raped and killed Lynn and Theresa.

That's when it struck me. I'd forgotten. Theresa was raped and killed. But why? Two women connected to the same group. Two women and one man. What was the connection? And if it was a possible series of murders done by

105

the same party, who would be next? I'd have to see Linda Clifford again. Before it was too late!

The thought left me with mixed reactions. She was, for one thing, a very beautiful woman; plus, she'd been a real whiz in the bedroom—what little I could remember about her during that drugged state.

I would have to see Linda Clifford if for nothing else other than to let her know about Theresa and the possible chance that it was a series of murders connected with the group Lynn had run around with and that she might be one of the next to die. Assuming it was a series of murders all interconnected—I would not want to be in her place.

Quickly, I turned the car off the freeway and headed in the direction of Linda Clifford's apartment. It was only a five-minute drive from where I'd made the turnoff.

I knocked at her door. There was no answer. So I tried again. Nobody answered.

Defeated, I returned to the car and started driving to my own apartment. I arrived there twenty minutes later. Walked up to my rooms.

The door was open. That was shock number one. The second shock was seeing Barbara lying in the middle of the front room. Her back was toward me.

Frantically I moved over to her, my temples throbbing in terrified agony. I couldn't think of anything but that Barbara, dear Barbara, had ended like Lynn and Theresa.

Then as I knelt down beside her, something hit my head. My last thought before the world spun around into a dizzy bottomless abyss, was that it was happening again within just a few hours. And even as that thought was starting to fade I had this numbing confusion. I wasn't sure that I was thinking of being knocked out again or worrying about Barbara's still form. Another murder?

That's when I realized that I was coming out of the daze. How long I'd been out I didn't know. But the last thoughts I had before losing consciousness, and the first one upon coming to, seemed to blend into one continuous concept.

Quickly, I turned. Barbara was still lying on the floor, right next to where I'd fallen.

106

Oh, God, don't take her, too!

The pain at the back of my head didn't bother me too much, now. I was more concerned about Barbara. The first thing I looked for was the sign of any sex violence.

I turned her over to discover that she was breathing evenly.

Thank God for small favors.

There didn't seem to be any indication that her clothing had been touched. She looked merely asleep.

I breathed easier.

I checked her over and discovered what looked like a fairly bad lump on Barbara's head. From all appearances she had only been hit on the head with a heavy object. But that was enough. In fact, far too much.

Gently, I tried to revive her. It didn't do any good. I tried again. Still no response.

Standing, I went to the medicine cabinet in the bathroom. I came back to Barbara's still form with smelling salts. They didn't do any good either.

I tried damp rags. Still no reaction. By now, I was more than just concerned or terrified. Emotions were rushing through me that were all but overwhelming. Both anger and fear and a little sorrow. Terrible emotional pain.

All I could think about was getting a doctor to her—and fast! Before it might be too late. I had to get help.

The phone was in my hand. I didn't remember standing and walking over to it. I was dialing the police.

A minute after that I was sitting down on the floor next to Barbara, holding her head in my arms.

How long I sat there I don't know. The next thing I was aware of was men in white suits moving around me. Voices talking. But I wasn't conscious of what they were saying at first.

Then there were men in police uniforms. Flashing camera bulbs. Questions. I answered them. I don't even know what I was saying. Words. People. Action. Lights.

But nothing mattered. Even my obsession to find Lynn's murderer seemed to have faded in importance. All I could think of was Barbara. If she hadn't come over that morning to help me clean my room, this wouldn't have happened to her. All I was concerned with was getting her well. Doing everything I could do.

And worst of all I didn't want to admit that I was in love. Yet that was the only explanation. The only possible logical reason for my reaction.

They let me ride in the ambulance with Barbara. My eyes didn't leave her face. A face so beautiful to me, now, that it made me want to cry. A face, still and quiet. I didn't allow myself to think that it might never again smile or laugh or tease. That she might never again know the thrill of a lover's touch. That I would never hold her dear form in my arms. Never have a chance to tell her how much I loved her.

☞Chapter Thirteen☜

The thoughts that run through a man's mind in times of stress are amazing. A complete change can alter your approach to life and living. One moment you think one thing, the next you doubt all those solid convictions. You start seeing things from a different angle.

Sitting in the hospital, waiting to find out just how serious Barbara's injury was, I began to do a lot of thinking about myself and life and the past. The future. Where was I headed? Why had Barbara gotten herself into such a situation that had put her in the hospital? And where would it all end?

Questions upon questions. Just the asking them created new puzzles.

I'd been bumming around all my life. After high school I went to college. Then the war. And I was in the thick of it. Seeing violence at every turn. Death.

For one reason or another—I couldn't remember now—I managed to get myself re-enlisted. And then after that, in Japan, I managed to become involved with a few Japanese girls; one in particular, and then I took a third enlistment. Then out and home. Finding out about Lynn's lying style. Continuing to bum around. And for what purpose? Another broad in bed. Another quick thrill. Another momentary interlude to help me escape from facing my future, my life and my existence! A nobody. A bum who ran from woman to woman. From meaningless job to meaningless job.

But that was only a small part of my worries or concern. It was an undercurrent running through every thought, but silently.

There were three major items I was most concerned

with.

One: Would Barbara be safe?

Two: Who had done that to her? The same person who had hit me?—No doubt! The same person that was in my apartment the night before? Maybe.

Three: What connection did all this have to the rape and killing of both Lynn and Theresa? And if it did—why hadn't Barbara been killed and raped?

And still another idea and emotional problem was hammering through my awareness: *why the hell had I fallen so hard for Barbara?*

Not, mind you, that she wasn't one hell of a lady. But for me to realize, so suddenly, how important she really was to me. That, alone, was stunning.

Nothing made sense. Nothing added up—except in the form of a headache. This was the mixed confusion of my thoughts.

One of the doctors noticed the wound on the back of my head and examined it. It was nothing serious but he still had insisted getting on an x-ray of it. After that, the matter was dropped. Apparently I was still in good health.

Then the questions of the police reporter. He wanted to know everything. And now, sitting in the hospital, I was beginning to wonder exactly what I had told him. How much? And what? The daze muddying my conscious thinking also clouded over the fractured events in the hospital now. The doctors, technicians, reporters—all, just a blur.

Things were clearing. They were clearing much too fast and too soon. I couldn't handle them, logically. Emotionally, I couldn't work them out. Everything was beginning to hit me all at once. My own inability to find the man who had started this whole nightmare. My emotional reaction toward Barbara; my normal fear and concern about her physical condition. Lynn's death. They all got tangled up in my mind.

That was another thing that struck me as being odd. Lynn's death had suddenly dropped in importance. And that had two reactions on me. One of guilt; the other, puzzlement. How could I possibly find myself feeling less concern about the fact that Lynn had ended the way she had? And now, the

110

danger to Barbara? Maybe because Barbara was still alive. Maybe because the girl you have suddenly discovered you love is more important than a sister whom you have loved all your life. Coupled with the fact that Lynn and myself had not really been socially close during the last months.

A lot of questions. It seemed to me that all I was doing the last couple of days was asking questions and getting no answers.

And then another little hammer tapped at the back of my head.

If Barbara comes out of this okay...what then?

Fun and games was one thing. But in a serious relationship life changes dramatically. I could hardly consider coupling with any woman like her without being able to offer some kind of stable future. And my past was not a good recommendation for a supportive husband.

That reality shocked me on several levels. At the same time, it didn't matter if Barbara would want me or not—would any woman want a bum? No future in that.

Up until now, in my life, I'd just managed to survive from month to month, year to year. There was the military pension, of course. I'd had some minor medical problems coming out of combat and then, too, there were some investments that had panned out over the years. Nothing major; nothing much with a great, grand future. I'd just managed to stumble through life. With no real ultimate goal.

Lynn had stumbled into a death trap. What were the dreams and goals that were shattered for her by a perverted rape artist?

I pulled my thoughts away from her and back to Barbara. If she turned out okay, if she lived, if she wanted me, if...if and if...what could I offer her in return? Thrills and fun was one thing between two swinging singles looking for nothing but an active social life. A married couple would need to expect much more.

Sure, my immediate job was fine. Writing was a nice way to make a living, even free-lancing. Or just working for a paper, which I'd done in the past. But was it enough?

I could, of course, take all my investments and channel them into some kind of business thing. I wasn't stupid.

111

And Barbara wasn't a dummy, either. She'd been in real estate and even selling insurance. In fact, from every indication I'd seen, she was one whiz on many levels. But I could hardly consider living off her—though in a partnership we might manage some kind of successful business venture.

My mind swam in distorted images, back and forth, past and present and future.

All of them were escape traps from reality. The past was done with. The future was unknown. Only the present had meaning.

Then again, my thoughts returned to the real problems at hand.

Maybe Theresa had been right. Maybe Barbara had been right. Maybe Lt. Johnson had been right. Maybe everybody had been right—except me.

Maybe I should have left matters alone. Kept out of it all. Let the police take care of the rape artist.

Still, would that have kept the person, whoever they might be, from searching my apartment and then returning?

And why was anybody searching my apartment? That was another question. What were they looking for? And what connection—what possible connection—could it have with the rapes?

That's when Lt. Johnson's voice broke into my thoughts. "Well, hello, so now we meet again!" The tone had an edge of impatience to it, shaded with sarcasm. "It seems like you follow this whole case around like it was glued to your ass."

I looked up. He was standing over me, his eyes dark and tired looking. Long lines were under them. "And just what are you doing here, Mr. Matson?"

"I might ask that same question of you!" I snapped back. I wasn't really mad at him and I don't believe that he really was snapping out at me. Just that both of us were seeing the same frustration which we each felt inside.

He relaxed and almost smiled. "I guess it's been pretty hard on you."

"Yeah." I let it lay there. But he picked it up.

"Okay. Mind telling me all about it?"

"This?"

"Nothing else. I just got a call that the person involved this time was here. We think it has connections with the other two."

"No rape this time!"

"Oh?" He looked surprised. "Well, I didn't even have a chance to check the report. Just was sent here fast!"

The doctor came up then. His face was heavy and serious looking. "Which one of you is... oh, you must be Mr. Matson."

He turned toward me.

"How is she?"

He was silent for a moment and then said: "She's going to be all right. Just a bad fracture."

"Just a bad fracture?" I bellowed, feeling my insides do a tailspin. "I thought that..."

"Oh...I'm sorry. Not exactly what I meant." He smiled slightly. "Actually minor—by that I mean she'll be okay. Just in the hospital for a day or so. By bad I simply meant that's what kept her out so long. She's conscious now..."

"Can I...?"

"Go on in. Room 4E. She's waiting for you."

He directed me to her room. Then he started talking to Lt. Johnson who was questioning him.

I didn't even hear anything they said. Only one thought was running through my mind. To see Barbara. To tell her that I loved her. To be near her. Say I'd always be near her. So many things which were suddenly welling up through me, taking complete control of my every thought and emotion. It didn't even occur to me to think of it as being rather odd or sudden—or that she might not return my love. It didn't even seem strange that I was abruptly freely admitting to myself that I was in love and willing to let the world know about it.

That's what happens to a person when they are pushed sideways through a knot-hole. That's the way I felt. Suddenly everything was centering on Barbara and myself. The two of us, together. Just to be with her, alone, to hold her dear sexy form against my body, to feel the softness of this...

I let the image fade.

Then I was standing over her bed. Looking down at her. Smiling like a fool. Our eyes were locked in an embrace, that silent awareness which sometimes takes place between two people. For some reason I felt that I didn't have to tell her that I loved her. I had the idea that she somehow knew. How, I didn't know. But sometimes women are like that. They can tell about things, about love, about men.

Still, I had to tell her. Even if it wasn't necessary, I had to know. I had to express myself, regardless.

I reached for her hand and the fingers clasped mine tightly.

"How are you?" I asked, almost choking with my own emotion.

She laughed, lightly. "Don't be silly!"

"Silly?"

"Just a bump on the head! That's all."

"You know who did it?"

She slowly moved her head from side to side.

I asked: "How?"

"When I got there your door was open. I walked in and—bang."

"Just like last night. The same way it happened to me."

She smiled quietly. Her eyes hadn't left mine.

I squeezed her hand. "I'll make this up to you. Some how..." I promised, lamely. The words that were flying through my mind just wouldn't form on my tongue. Not fear, just lack of a way to say them.

She merely looked up at me and lovingly said: "You have."

"What?"

"Made it up to me. By just being here, like this."

Her eyes closed. Her hand relaxed its grip on mine. "I'm a little tired, I guess. That blow did something to me... Guess I might as well take advantage of it."

Her eyes opened once more and then she smiled again. "Let the police take care of it...*please?*"

I didn't make any attempt to answer that request. It was impossible to say I wouldn't do anything about what had happened to her, to Lynn and to poor emotionally mixed up Theresa. I couldn't promise her anything of the kind, and she seemed to realize what my silence meant. Her fingers slid away from mine and the smile froze into a stiff frightened expression.

"You going to…?"

"I don't know what I'm going to do. But I can't just sit around and do nothing. Twice somebody has been trying to hit a home run with my head. They almost made it with you. Another person—maybe the same one—killed Lynn and now Theresa DeBray."

Her eyebrows arched weakly at the name of Theresa. I quickly explained who the other woman was. Only then did her face relax. But the concern or worry hadn't left.

We were silent for a moment and then the nurse came in.

"Time's up!" the woman smiled, as if she thought of herself as something of a comic relief.

"We have to have our shot now," she announced to Barbara.

"What?" I asked.

"Just normal hospital operating procedure. This young lady took quite a bump."

I leaned over and kissed Barbara on the lips. She attempted to respond weakly.

"We gave her a shot to relieve the pain," the nurse explained. "That makes her a little sleepy, you know."

I hadn't known. "When can she get out?"

"Oh, I wouldn't know about that. You'd have to ask the doctor."

I left her room and walked down the hall.

Lt. Johnson was waiting where I had left him.

The doctor had left. For the first time since I'd met him I was almost glad he was there.

I stopped in front of the police officer. For a moment there didn't seem to be anything to say. I knew what was going on in his mind. He wanted to know if I'd found out anything but he was a little embarrassed about asking. It was one of those times when the right thing seemed the wrong thing; when the normal was abnormal.

Taking out a pack of cigarettes, he offered me one.
"Thanks."

After lighting them, he asked, "Mind if I ask you a few questions?"

For a moment I didn't answer him. Looking back I guess that this was when I finally changed my attitude toward Johnson. The very fact that he was a little hesitant about barging right into the subject said a lot about the kind of human being he was. I hadn't taken the time to notice before.

I stood there for a little while and then sighed, attempting a weak smile. "Okay, Johnson, you win."

"What?"

"Mind if we talk over a drink?"

He just nodded and followed me out of the hospital. Down the street there was a bar, toward which we walked in pensive silence. I didn't feel like talking, yet. I was saving it for after the first drink. I needed something to calm my roughened nervous system. I also needed time to think things over.

Up to this point I'd been acting pretty childish toward the police. And even worse, I'd been pretty childish about myself.

Maybe there wasn't anything wrong in my wanting to do some private investigating on my own. But there was no reason to act as if the police force was some evil enemy. They were, like Johnson had said before, on my side. At least I could cooperate with them. I could give what little information I could.

We arrived at the bar. He pointed toward a corner of the bar where a booth was set off alone.

"Over there?"

I just nodded. A moment later we were seated with a bartender standing over us.

"Make mine scotch," I told the man, looked over at the lieutenant. He shook his head. "Nothing. On duty. Do you have coffee?"

The man looked sour, but nodded and left.

"I guess we've had quite a bad start, haven't we, Matson?"

116

"That's one way of putting it." I nervously fingered a small book of matches.

"Been quite a blow to you? All this happening?"

I nodded again.

"Well don't think the police force isn't aware of what a shock things like that can be to people. Sure, we get a little numbed to the brutalities of life. Death is a part of our business. But also life is an important part of our business. Something like this is an exciting newspaper story to the guy on the street. But I guess you know all about the newspaper scene."

I nodded again, said absently: "I've seen a lot of things, but when it hits home it is something different, believe me!"

"I believe you. It is the same way me. Every day I face one kind of violent crime or death. It becomes impersonal. I see sudden suffering and loss brought to strangers by other strangers. I watch and don't let it hurt me, personally. But to be truthful don't know how I'd feel if something like what happened to your sister and these others should happen to my own daughter. The idea is frightening. I've tried to imagine my reactions; guess they'd be something like yours. I'd be in a blind kind of fury. I don't think I'd be able to really let the law handle matters. At least my first reaction would be such pure insanity. But that's not the answer. The law is better set up for handling such matters and they do it in their own, slow, but sure way."

He hesitated and then said: "What I'm trying to get across is that maybe we don't seem quite human, because we're exposed to this kind of thing every day of the week. But it has nothing to do with our emotional, personal side. We have loves and hates just as strong as the next person does. The vast majority of guys working on the force are loyal, hard-driving men, trying to protect society against itself. There are a few that go bad, take pay-offs, do a little dirty dealings of their own, get a little rough when it isn't called for. But a few bad ones don't make the whole barrel rotten. Just like a few sick blacks don't make the whole race bad. The ghetto problems are another issue. And a lot of otherwise good officers get pretty damned prejudice and big-

117

oted, cause they see the bad side, not the human issues involved. It is all too easy to ignore everything but the blueline. And some cops, quite frankly, don't see the people they are supposed to be serving. Maybe we should be cycled every five years or so…another problem…never mind that. But what I'm saying is, with all its faults, it's the best we can do. And to be truthful I know more good police officers than bad apples.

"The thing is, Matson, don't get the idea that I don't care. If I let myself be really touched by these things I'd be all tied up in knots. A quick basket case for the madhouse. I have to keep myself as detached as possible from what I'm doing. Once the emotions get involved I'm not doing a good job. And maybe the methods we use seem cruel at the time, but in the long run it is the results that count. My job is to catch a brutal sex fiend who is having a field day with a lot of young women. The important thing is to stop him before more women end up like your sister. She was only the first— those others left friends and relatives who are just as sick about this thing as you are!"

He abruptly fell silent, letting me take in what he had said.

It was a long silence. Then the drinks came. I ordered another before the man could leave. Downing half the scotch I looked directly at Lt. Johnson.

He really wasn't such a bad guy. Even considering that he'd been pretty rough on me. Using me as a guinea pig. But in a way I'd gotten exactly what I deserved. He'd given me a chance to come right out and tell him all that I knew the first time I'd met him. After that he'd done things the hard way.

A good man to have on the force, I realized. A good man to have working on my side. Tough, when it was necessary. Easy going when he could get away with it. Quiet and careful when the time called for that type of action.

All in all, he'd only responded to me and the facts as they presented themselves to him. I'd called the punches. The only thing was that his hits had been harder, because he had a much longer and stronger *arm*.

But it was more than that. Here was a man who willingly let me name the time and place. Coming to the bar. Knowing that maybe it would be easier for me to talk then, while he could, with all legal rights, take me to the station for questioning, force me to talk under the threat of holding me in jail.

No. Actually he'd been more than open and fair with me. It was about time that I played ball with the police.

After a deep sigh, I told him everything, leaving nothing out except my private affairs. When it came to Linda Clifford I told the whole thing. His expression became mildly surprised at my frankness and at the woman's boldness. I didn't leave a thing out because I suddenly realized that anything and everything might be a possible clue. He just sat there quietly listening, taking it all in, in detail.

Afterwards he just nodded, paid the bill for my three drinks and asked me to come with him.

MURDER TIMES FOUR, BY CHARLES NUETZEL

☛Chapter Fourteen☚

Working with the police instead of against them was going to turn out to be completely different than I had imagined. Not that I hadn't given up the idea of personal satisfaction when it came to the guy who had killed my sister so brutally and used Barbara and myself as batting balls. But it was only a case of discovering that, with the police's help, I would get things done much faster; more safely.

My first reaction, when deciding to play ball with Lt. Johnson, was to help him out—but not necessarily give up my own personal hopes of getting the bastard who was responsible for what had been happening the last couple of days. It was Sunday and the next day I was supposed to go to work on the paper. I had one of those nice jobs which were eight hours a day, nine to six, five days a week, no more! My job wasn't so important that it couldn't be handled in those hours; and I was too important at the paper to be pushed around.

That meant that I'd have to run down the man before work started—or miss out. But there was another time limit. That was getting the man before he got to anybody else. Of course, that was the police's concern, more than mine. My only wish was simply to get the bastard between my fingers so that I would have the privilege of squeezing the life out of him. My total conviction had become obsessive. In my mind, this was the only solution.

It was a funny thing. Here I was, helping the police force, yet even with a stronger determination to get at the man first. There were several reasons for both decisions. The important thing now was to get the man stopped. What he had done to Barbara could be done to anybody—what he had

121

done to Lynn and Theresa could be done to a number of people. The thing was to stop the man before he had a chance to continue whacking people around.

So Linda Clifford would be the next stop.

We went to her apartment right after leaving the bar. She wasn't in. We talked to the manager and he told us that she had left earlier that morning. But he didn't know where or when she'd be back.

"And that leaves us where?" Johnson asked once we were back in his squad car. I silently shook my head. That left us any place—which meant; *nowhere!*

In a way, I was glad we hadn't found her. I had the idea that maybe it had been a mistake mentioning her name to Johnson. If I could get to her first, by myself, I couldn't help thinking I'd get better results. Maybe I was wrong about that—but I wanted the chance to prove it.

The first thing that I needed to concentrate on was getting by myself. With Johnson, I couldn't possibly run down a couple of leads. I was sure they would get me further if he weren't along. I'd told him about them but he said that they had already been followed.

One was the strip joint on the matchbook cover that Lynn had had in her apartment. The other was the restaurant. The leads might be dead—but I couldn't help thinking there might be something to discover there. At least I could satisfy my own doubts by checking.

And then there was Eddy DeBray.

The police still considered him as a prime suspect. I couldn't, as yet, think of any motive.

Even though he had given some minor indication of mental derangement. Minor or not, the man was on my list of possible suspects.

Still, things weren't going to work out as easily as I'd thought.

The radio in the car made a crackling noise and then a voice called for Lt. Johnson. The report was that another raped, dead woman had been found.

My throat choked. The first thought was that it might be Linda Clifford.

Johnson looked at me as he started the engine. "I'll

122

have to take you along. Afterwards I'll return you to the hospital and your car."

"You couldn't keep me away!" I told him, snuffing out the cigarette butt in the ashtray. "You don't think that it might be the Clifford girl, do you?"

He just shrugged and headed the car into traffic. About ten minutes later we arrived at a small two-story private home. Police cars, an ambulance, newspaper reporters and neighbors were crowded around the front lawn.

I followed Johnson through the crowd. For one glorious moment I felt like somebody important—on official business. Everybody made way for us.

A moment later we were inside the house. A few quick questions sent us into an upper bedroom where a quite attractive woman lay in a pool of red blood. She was dead. Any resemblance between the dead girl and Linda Clifford was only the fact that she ran around in the same gang. We didn't discover that until some time later after a lot of questions.

She had been raped and killed. Nobody had been at the house except herself when it happened. She was the daughter of a rich businessman. Her parents hadn't discovered her until this morning.

There weren't any clues as to who might have done the killing. The whole thing made me slightly sick and I asked Lt. Johnson if I might leave. He seemed glad to get rid of me.

A phone call got me a cab within minutes. And a little later I was at the hospital. A few questions got me to the doctor who was attending Barbara.

"How is she?" I was quick to ask.

He smiled and told me that things were a lot less serious than they had originally thought. Then he explained her condition in a lot of medical mumbo-jumbo, which went over my head. But the facts were simple: she would be out by the next day; all she needed was to take care of herself for a while—and not get any more hits on the head.

I told him I'd pick her up the next day, then went to my car. There were several things that I wanted to take care of in the next few hours. One was finding Linda Clifford, if I had to wait at her apartment.

A little later I was knocking on her door. A voice answered. I just knocked again. I was afraid she might not be so anxious to answer the door if she knew it was me.

The door opened and her head peeked out. The door started to close but I held it open, pushing it inward. The struggle was short and I won. I don't believe that she really put her full effort into the matter; it seemed pretty easy to get in.

"What the hell are you doing in here?" she demanded, placing her fists on her hips.

All I could do was gulp.

She was standing before me all but nude, a towel pulled tight about her body. Her lips half smiled as she noticed the surprised expression on my face.

"You like me?" she laughed, almost tauntingly. "I knew you liked me!"

The words were those of a person who had suddenly learned that they have won a battle they didn't really know had been theirs. The tone was throaty. Her eyes sparkled and the mad fury had left.

"Want a drink?" she asked, starting to walk over to the bar, holding the towel in place. "Or something else?"

I wanted one but didn't want to take the chance of having her drug me into a sexual stupor again.

When I didn't answer she turned and looked at me.

"You look as if you need one." Her lips smiled as her eyes took in every inch of my face and body. The examination was meant to imply only one thing.

"Why don't you get dressed?" I suggested. It upset me quite a bit that the only thing that seemed to run around in her brain was sex. Every glance, every look, every action cried out sensually to me. And nothing else.

"Why?" she laughed. "Don't you like me this way? Don't you want to touch me?"

"Damn it all, I'll take that drink!" I snapped, walking over to the bar. "But I'll fix it myself if you don't mind!"

"Help yourself."

I poured a drink and tried to think things out. I'd come here for one thing: to get information from this over-sexed nymph. Not to talk sex. Yet her words had caused an automatic physical reaction.

The trouble with us guys is that we're rather basic and primitive. Somebody had once said a "prick has no conscience or morality!" I'm not quite certain how he meant that, a universal statement about men or just nasty men at large. But it was true. A man's body responded without any permission from his mind.

"I have a few questions I want to ask you," I told her, taking a swallow of the drink in my hands. "I want the answers, this time!"

She was smiling strangely, as if she had some secret she was keeping to herself.

"So, question away."

"Won't you please get dressed?" I almost begged. "I'll have to admit—if that's what you're after—that you're beautiful, sexy, desirable and all that. I can't think straight with well, you know! All…that!"

She laughed. This time it was deep and throaty. "It's my apartment. You came in—against my will—so you can just do your damn questioning with me dressed any way I damn please. Or totally naked!"

She walked over to the sofa and lay down on her back. Her body arranged itself in such a way as to show off every sensual grace of her figure.

One pull on that towel and she'd be naked as hell.

I didn't look in her direction. Instead I kept my eyes on the floor or the glass in my hand.

The liquor felt good. It soothed some of my raw nerves. It relaxed me. I took another swallow of it.

I heard a light giggle from Linda. My eyes automatically turned in her direction and that throaty sound. Her lips opened wide in a loud laugh.

"What's so damn funny?"

"You'll find out. You'll find out!"

I dropped my eyes from that obscene sight.

"What's wrong, big boy? Can't you look at Linda?" She laughed again. "I bet you change your mind, later. I bet you do!"

"Cut it out!"

"Okay, ask away. Anything!"

I thought for a moment and then took another drink of the whiskey. It burned through me. This time the effect was startlingly stimulating. It made my mind clear and I knew, suddenly, where to start; what questions to ask first; what I had to know.

"Have you seen Eddy DeBray lately?" I asked, finding it hard not to look in her direction.

"Oh, Eddy-boy. He called last night. But I was on my way out. We have a date for tonight!"

I looked up at her in sudden alarm. "Don't make it!"

She wiggled nervously.

"Why not?"

I started to explain but the words wouldn't come out. I found myself looking deep into her eyes. The words were frozen in my throat. My head was spinning dizzily. My throat tight. My heart, an explosive hammer in my lungs.

Such a beautiful sight, my mind cried as I downed another swallow of the whiskey So wonderfully beautiful So delightfully sensual So willing and able. Just throbbing with life and eager passion. Just one tug of that towel and her body would be mine for the taking.

My mind froze at that thought. Shocked at what I was thinking. I downed another large swallow of the drink. Then emptied it.

"Like what you're seeing?" she inquired. "Want to see more? I don't mind. I just love it when a man looks at me like that. Turns me crazy all inside. Makes me want to get him in my arms. So, look away."

The blood was racing faster and faster through me. It was harder and harder to keep from looking at Linda.

I needed another drink. Something to take my mind away from her sexual beauty.

"You don't mind?" I asked about the drink I was pouring. I realized that the question was not necessary but I had to say something at the time.

"Sure, help yourself!"

I refused to look at her for a long time. Just sipped the drink. Took time to think. Time to organize my thoughts. Time to attempt to return them to the subject of Eddy

DeBray.

"What do you know about Eddy?" I asked, finally.

"Oh, he's a *real* man! He doesn't need any help to be interested in girls—like some men I've known. He takes a girl in his arms and makes love to her the way a woman likes to feel a man. He knows how to please a woman. How to caress her. The way he puts his hands all over me…right down and dirty. Oh, so delicious. His lips smother into me so hot and open. I can almost feel his tongue in me, right now. Oh…it makes me so hot. So terribly hot all over!"

"Knock it off!" I yelled. The sound of my voice shattered through the room like gunshot.

The shocked silence that followed was numbing.

Finally I said, "Just answer the questions in a simple statement."

"Look!" she snapped angrily, "I'm not on the witness stand! You're no damn cop. I'll answer the questions any way I damn well please. If you like it or not!" Then her voice changed. "Why don't you come over here and talk to me. I won't bite. After all, I'm a grown woman. I liked being touched by you. I think you could be a real lover if you half tried. Think how much fun it would be to put your hand here … really deep."

"Stop!" My mind was crying to walk over to her and take her in my arms. I was holding the glass frantically, almost crushing it in my violence.

"Oh, don't be a shit. You want me. You know you want me. You can't help but want me. You remember how it was before. So lovely. So hot and…. Come on over here and let me have…what you're hiding there…." She laughed in delight at her own words. "Oh, yes, come on over and show me your pride and joy. I really want you…"

Her voice was both passionate and on the level of a monotone.

"I want you to touch me here and there and everywhere. I want to feel your body, I want to have my hands running all over you, and wrap my fingers around you, and let my lips discover you and just stroke and kiss and…"

The continued, rhythmically pulsing as her eyes continued to feast on what she so wanted to have, hold, devour, possess, ravish.

It was hypnotic.

"About Eddy DeBray!" I asked, trying hard to keep my mind on the subject. "He's a dangerous man."

"Don't I know it!" she laughed. "Any girl who gets near him is sure to lose her virtue. Assuming she has one."

"He's wanted by..."

"Every girl who wants a *real* man. All but me. Not right now. Right now I want you. Oh, how I want to feel your lips on mine. I need you..."

Her words were my thoughts spoken. It was crazy. I felt as if I was in a whirling pool, the world spinning around and around, whipping me in its mad current, helpless to fight back.

The desperate driving need to take this woman was suddenly so overwhelming that all other thoughts seemed distant. I heard her voice drumming on, murmuring on, offering, and promising all kinds of erotic pleasures. And each verbal offer was like a caress working over my body.

I simply found it impossible to control my will. I was clutched in the vice of her voice, her suggestions. My eyes were frozen to her curving form, so willingly offering itself to the carnal passions of my own body.

"Let me have you," she murmured over and over. The towel seemed to have slipped slightly and she smiled in satisfaction as my eyes just stared hungrily.

Nothing made sense other than accepting this woman's demanding offer. Yet it was insane.

"Come on over here ... so we can really ... know one another the way we did before. But better this time."

I tried to tell myself that it would be degenerate to give in to her commands—for commands they were.

I attempted to argue that it didn't make sense for her to be making such blunt offers. Even if we'd screwed the hell out of one another already.

What kind of woman would let herself become the plaything to any man willing to climb into bed with her? What kind of sick perverted being could act like this?

I'd known enough women in my life to understand the basic drives of the human flesh; to realize there were all kinds of perverse minds. I had escaped into the arms of many willing females I hardly knew while in the service. But it was different. I'd been the aggressive male on the make; the woman was the submissive object of my own personal cravings and chase.

There were ground-rules that even the lowest tramp would follow. There were the drinks at some bar, conversation and then the subtle suggestion of going some place else. Those were the rules everybody followed. The flirtations which led to sexual passes.

At least everybody I'd known before followed some pattern of those rules. Until now and coming in contact with this sex-web of willing young things throwing themselves before men like mindless sexual machines without any sense of morality.

My eyes kept looking at her, examining every curve and depression of her lovely form under the white bath towel. I wanted to go over there and yank it off her body. I wanted to do nothing short of ravishing her to madness.

I kept thinking how easy it would be to strip that towel away.

There wasn't any real passion, only a numbed awareness that there could be no escape for me.

Then I was walking toward the sofa. It didn't seem strange any more: just logical. I wasn't thinking about anything but total possession of Linda.

"Oh, yes, that's good!" she murmured, just ripping the towel off her body. She squirmed in delight, reaching out for me.

Suddenly I was leaning toward her. Our lips met and I was pulled down into the demanding embrace of her savage animal fury.

Her hands were all over me, reaching, clawing, searching, and helping me undress. Then, when I was stripped naked, her fingers squeezed on me in such a voluptuous manner that I could do nothing but react. From then on she was a furious guide that drove me into a consuming fiery hell. I was only able to follow the mad series of continued kissing, caressing and finally powerful thrusting that took total possession of our bodies. We became completely fused into one unified act of torrid ecstatic bliss.

☛Chapter Fifteen☚

This wasn't the time to be intimate with any woman, let alone Linda Clifford. But that didn't occur to me in the least. My only concern was the craving burn that was welling through my body like a never-ending fire. Where it had come from it didn't even seem to matter; I didn't even make any attempt to question it. There it was, and it had to be soothed. And it didn't stop after the first hungry union.

She refused to stop.

"Oh," she murmured, eyes feasting on me in wonder. "You're so hot!"

She once again was all over me. We were lying on the floor, stark naked and her hands and lips began to travel along my body so frantically that all I could do was react to her voluptuous kisses.

It was like climbing a gigantic mountain with rugged, earthquake-tortured sides. A raw, distant, out-of-focus world of colors and sharp sensations.

Then I reached the top and without warning, the world spun into nothingness. I was falling downwards into an angry sea of molten hot lava that surged around me in a frantic attempt to burn the very skin from my body

The world seemed to dim and blackness formed before my tired vision. I heard movement. But that was all.

The sleep lasted forever. A nightmare of female hips, yielding breasts; movement; hazy erotic pleasure. Even in that relaxed exhaustion the symbols seemed to work my body and nerves until I woke up gasping in terror.

The woman was lying next to me. We were in her bed. How we had gotten there I didn't know. But one thought shot through my body and mind: somehow she had managed to drug me again.

Blind fury overcame me then. I was half-insane with anger. This little bitch had somehow managed to get at me again, just for the joy of satisfying her body; a body that was abnormally lacking in the finer instincts.

She stirred. Her eyes opened. Her lips smiled.

"Hello, lover-man." Her arms went up and encircled my neck. "You want some more fun? I can't get enough of you in me!"

That's when sanity left me for a terrible moment. Anger. Madness. Fury. Hate. All of it welled up into being; full force. All the agony which I'd gone through in these last two days suddenly burst outwards at this helpless woman.

I swung and my hand slashed across that lovely face. Her head whipped to one side, following the direction and impact of the blow.

My arm swung back again and her head turned once more.

"You little bitch!" The words shot out of my mouth, uncontrolled.

She was laughing. A small trickle of blood was showing itself at the side of her mouth. But she was laughing. At first I thought she was hysterical; then I realized the truth.

She had liked it! She was enjoying herself, now. She waited for the next slap.

Her eyes were closed and her mouth relaxed. A shiver of wanton pleasure raced through that body as if she were in an orgasmic fit.

I looked down at her in horror and disgust. I could not believe my eyes. It didn't seem possible that a person would actually enjoy being beaten up. I'd heard about it. Read about it—but never had I seen anyone like her.

I wanted to vomit. The acid was working its way up from my stomach.

"What are you waiting for?" she whispered through cut lips. "Don't stop. I'm dying for me!"

I leaped frantically from the bed and ran toward the bathroom.

A little later I returned, feeling better. I was still violently upset—mentally, physically and emotionally. I'd never hit a woman like that before. There had been good cause; but I'd never done it before and I was mentally disgusted with myself. I was sick emotionally and physically about Linda Clifford. That anybody could be like her seemed incredible. She was a sickened blotch on the record of humanity. People like her, I realized, should be put away. They didn't have a right to be out in society to contaminate the decent people.

And I realized that little sister Lynn must have been very much like Theresa and Linda. And that was more than horrible.

Getting dressed, I tried to do my best to ignore Linda. My first reaction was to warn her once more about Eddy DeBray. But I thought better of it. If I told her what I thought might be the truth, she just might warn Eddy. The only thing that I could do now was to get Lt. Johnson. Tell him that Eddy and Linda were supposed to have a date that evening and maybe the police would set a trap for him.

I suddenly didn't want any part of it. All I wanted to do was to get away from everything and anything that had to do with Lynn and her past and her life.

I would, I realized, be around to see that Eddy DeBray was caught. That was one thing that I promised myself. But I realized, also, that I couldn't really do it all by myself. I'd need help.

The important thing was to get Eddy behind bars or dead. For the present, at least, the revenge had been burned out of me. Linda had burned it completely out—all my emotions, except disgust.

Later they would return; but right now all I could think of was getting out of her apartment. It had an evil smell about it. A sickened air that wouldn't leave my nostrils until I was somewhere else.

"What are you doing?" Linda asked, sitting up in bed. "You aren't going to leave?"

"You're damned right!"

"Why don't you have a drink first. I bet that will make you change your mind."

That's when it struck me. The liquor. That's what had

done it.

"Take a dive, baby!" I snapped, walking out of the apartment.

I needed the fresh air. It helped to revive my tired muscles. It cleared the numbness in my brain. The dopey feeling was still there, but a quick walk around the block in search of a telephone made me feel better. Once in the telephone booth, I called the police, asking for Lt. Johnson. He wasn't in. So I left the message for him that Eddy DeBray was supposed to have a date with Linda Clifford that evening.

At the moment I felt hungry and needed food. Walking to my car I started it up and headed down toward a restaurant that I knew about. It was cheap, quick and good.

All three of those considerations were important.

After a quick meal, I called the police station again.

Lt. Johnson still wasn't in but they would give him the message the moment he arrived. That was just great!

It was beginning to get on into the afternoon and I didn't know quite what to do. There were several possibilities; none of which appealed to me. Finally, I had to choose one. I drove my car up to the street where Linda Clifford lived, park it a couple of houses down, just close enough so that I'd see Linda Clifford coming out or Eddy DeBray going in.

Two ideas presented themselves to me, then. One, that Eddy might be at his home. But the police had it staked out. The other was that he might have already picked up Linda. I decided to call and find out if she was still in. The minute the phone rang I could easily hang up. Then it occurred to me that if I left the car and the position I was located at, Eddy might show up.

Somehow I had to find a way of seeing if she was in. Then I remembered the manager, Mr. Hanson. He might know if she had left. If not, maybe I could get him to do the phoning.

It was only a matter of a few minutes to find him. He was in his apartment-office. The moment the door opened, he recoiled, as if scared silly.

"Cool it! I need some help."

"Sure, sure," he said, as if saying quite the opposite.

"Look, this is important." I explained the situation to him, all the time his face contorted in a mixture of doubt and fear. But finally he seemed to relax and in the end actually became quite cooperative. By the time I was finished his eyes were wide and beady with alarm, but of a different kind.

"Don't you think that this is a matter for the police?" he asked.

"I've been trying to get them, but the lieutenant in charge of the case can't be contacted."

"That's strange..." he muttered almost to himself.

"Anyway, will you help?"

He nodded furiously. "I'll run up there. That way I can be sure that she's alone."

Five minutes later he returned.

"She's here. Alone." He smiled nervously.

"Want to wait here in the office? I could keep the door half open and you would be able to see anybody on their way to the stairs"

I nodded my thanks.

Scared little man though Mr. Hanson was, at least he was decent enough. Then a thought occurred to me. "Say, could you tell me who discovered the body of the man in Lynn's apartment?"

"Why I did."

"How s that?"

'Well, you left the place rather a mess So *I* went to the...well, you see, I always check throughout the apartment house every day. I was always especially interested in Miss Matson's apartment. And since I'd let you in and hadn't heard anything from you since then. Well so, now I checked. And as you know, the door was open, and, oh, what a mess! Then I saw this man laying face down in the middle of the room. Thought it was you; then noticed that he was smaller and had on a different colored suit. I didn't get any closer than trying to wake him. I was only a few feet from him when I saw the blood and the deep gash—it was horrible! I've never seen a dead man before, let alone that... well, anyway, I called the police. They came... and I guess you know the rest."

"Ever seen him before?"

He nodded. "He used to go to the parties your sister gave. Miss Clifford knew about him... they all ran around together. I knew the faces—but not the names."

I just sat, silently thinking over what he had said. Then thanked him. He left to take care of some sort of duties which he had, and then I just sat down, looking out through the half open door which gave a good view of the hallway.

I sat there, trying to think things out, organizing them in their proper order.

One: Lynn had been murdered and raped. Then Derk Meechan murdered in Lynn's apartment. After that, it was Theresa DeBray.

I'd first met Theresa in Lynn's apartment. She'd been looking for something. Then there was some unknown person who had played baseball with my head. I'd, no doubt, come in on them unexpectedly. Then they had panicked. Whacked me one and run. But why hadn't they taken the opportunity they had, while I was out cold, to search my room for whatever they were looking for? Why had they come back the next day?

Had they waited until I left?

Then another thought came home from a completely different direction. What if there had been two people? One last night, searching my room; the other in the morning. But that didn't make any sense. What motive?

And above all, what was anybody looking for? What could I have that would be of any interest?

Maybe they thought I'd found something in Lynn's apartment. That might explain it. So they had come to my place to look for it.

Theresa had been looking for something. Maybe for somebody else. Eddy? That was guess number one.

Okay, then. Maybe she hadn't found anything. Eddy gets mad at her for that reason or some other reason and kills her. Now he is faced with the idea that maybe I'd found what he was looking for.

But what could be so important as all that?

And why had Derk Meechan been killed?

My thoughts kept circling around and around. A puzzle without end. A mystery without a solution. The equation didn't add up to beans. Something was missing and I couldn't find out what.

Everybody who had been killed so far was connected with the group that Lynn ran around with.

Eddy had said something about Derk Meechan playing Lynn and Theresa against one another. That might give Theresa a motive to kill Derk. It might even give Eddy a motive to kill him. But the thing that bugged me was that no motive was all-conclusive to cover *all* the murders.

Maybe Derk Meechan had been an accident. But the point was, why had he been in Lynn's apartment in the first place, that late at night?

The thought occurred to me that maybe Theresa had been with Derk that evening when I'd first met her. Maybe he'd been the man in the car.

Then, after leaving, they had returned. Theresa had killed... But that didn't make any sense.

Eddy might have been there and killed Derk when he saw him with Theresa. Still, that seemed out of place.

Yet, considering that Eddy was a little unbalanced— that might be the clue.

My head was spinning with thoughts that had no connecting link.

I suddenly realized, there just wasn't a very strong case for Eddy being the killer. Not with the limited information I now had. The police thought he might be the man they were after. The only thing was, they couldn't possibly be sure... *unless!*

That's when I finally started to see a possible shape. A picture. The pieces were beginning to fit together. The trick, I realized, was to assume a certain fact that had to be proved and then see if there was any way of proving it. Not the reverse, like I'd been doing.

I had to start some place.

And when I did that, I suddenly saw that all the pieces could very easily fit around Eddy DeBray. That it would be simple for any D.A. to build up an ironclad case; assuming that the police had been able to track down the number of the license plate on the car I'd seen driving

137

Theresa away from the hotel the other evening.

Footsteps interrupted my thoughts.

My vision focused. Just in time. Eddy DeBray walked through the field of vision from the half open door where I sat, watching; waiting. Then he disappeared out of view. For a moment I didn't know what to do.

Quickly, I stepped over to the phone on the small desk in the corner. I dialed the police. It seemed to take forever.

Finally an answer. I got Lt. Johnson's department.

"Lieutenant Johnson in?"

"Sorry, he's still out

My mind was working frantically. Not even logically. The least I could have done was tell the officer the situation. He could have sent some police. That would have been better than nothing. But instead I reacted without thought. I replaced the receiver and walked out into the hall, toward the staircase, after Eddy.

☛Chapter Sixteen☚

I had hoped to get to Eddy before he got to Linda. The idea of having to face that woman again made me slightly nervous and ill at ease. But as it had turned out there wasn't anything I could do about it.

The door to Linda Clifford's apartment was just closing when I got up to it. Slightly breathless and now half scared to death, I barged in. The impact of the door opening abruptly pushed the two of them forward.

"What the hell!" Eddy cursed, turning.

Linda laughed happily. "It's fairy-boy! It's fairy-boy!"

Eddy DeBray looked at me for a long time. His eyes squinting as if he were attempting to recognize me; as if he had difficulty.

"Oh, you!" he finally exclaimed, smiling and extending his hand, "you're the *broad's* brother."

I didn't attempt to take the hand. Now, for the first time in hours, the burning hate was once again beginning to well into shape; an emotional black cloud was beginning to twist and turn inside my brain. Several mental reactions were taking place at one time. The hate and the fear. Terror and anger. The two of them left me momentarily weak and frozen helpless to the spot.

This was the moment I'd been waiting forever since I'd seen my sister's brutally beaten, raped and dead body in the morgue Friday night.

Her form faded and appeared and faded and appeared in front of Eddy. My head felt light and dizzy. Suddenly the world was spinning and I couldn't do anything about it. It was like being hit by all the emotional responses and hates

139

and fears, doubts and convictions. The exhaustion of running around like a madman; over-thinking; and worst of all, all the energy which had been drained out of me physically by the demanding passions and basic animal lusts of Linda Clifford.

The realization that the man who had started all this was standing now before me, just ready to have his life beaten out of him with my bare hands, left me completely drained.

"What's wrong with him?" I heard Eddy's voice ask the girl.

I couldn't answer. The black throbbing cloud had started ebbing around me like some monstrous life from another planet. It squeezed out all awareness.

I felt myself being lifted. Then I was being helped down on a bed. After that the world opened up and light appeared and sound returned.

"What hit you, old man?" Eddy asked, leaning over me. His face was bright and pleasant looking. "You been hitting the bottle, the rack—or both?"

Even the emotion was gone from me. I couldn't feel a thing. I knew that Eddy had been the one who had killed Lynn and all the others, but I couldn't feel anything.

I tried to sit up. He attempted to help.

"Get your damned hands off me!" I cursed.

"What's wrong with you, buddy?"

Right then I realized that actually there wasn't anything I could say. It might be possible to accuse him, but what good would that do? I couldn't prove anything. I might try beating his brains out, but how far would I get?

I looked at him for a long time.

"You're acting strangely—don't you feel right?"

"I feel like killing you. Mr. Rape Artist!"

He gulped at that. His eyes became beady; his forehead sweated, "What the hell are you talking about? What are you talking about?"

I was started now, and I realized that the only thing I could do was to continue with the bluff. "I'm afraid you slipped up a bit, Mr. DeBray."

"Come off it, man! I don't get it! Are you calling me

140

a rapist? Where do you get off calling *me*, Edward Phillip DeBray, a vile thing like that? I—I could..." He laughed then. His whole expression changed. "Boy, you had me going there. A real joker you are! A real joker." He patted me on the shoulder. I roughly brushed off his hand.

"What's the bit?" The eyes squeezed tightly as he looked at me more closely.

"I said that you killed my sister, Lynn. Then Theresa; and today you killed that woman in town and then you planned to take care of Linda, here, tonight."

"You're kidding!"

"Even if I was, the police aren't. They have conclusive proof that you are the man. The only thing I want to know is why? Why did you do it?

Even as I was speaking it seemed as if the whole scene had been clipped from a melodrama. In real life, things like this never happened—except maybe *once* in a lifetime. Another thing which I was aware of was the fact that what I was saying might not even be true; that maybe the police were onto the wrong man; that maybe I was wrong in having decided that Eddy was the rape artist. Maybe it was somebody who I didn't even know. And worst of all, maybe they actually didn't have any connection—which seemed unlikely.

He just laughed at me. "Boy, you sure must have a hangover! Man, what a story! What a story! You made it all up by yourself or did you get help? Help from that little bitch, Theresa? Or maybe from this tramp?"

He turned savagely toward Linda who, I noticed for the first time, was fully dressed.

"You did this to me!" he screamed, swinging his hand across her face. The impact of the blow almost sent her off her feet.

With an angry yell I reached for his shoulder, gripping it hard in my fingers. "Then it *was* you!"

"You kidding?" he laughed. The mood had changed once more. "You kidding me? Why would I do such a thing?"

"Yeah. You tell *me*! Why'?" My fingers gripped tighter on his arm.

141

He winced. "Come on. Let's quit the kidding. Let go. Please. Let go of my arm. *Please!*" His voice was pleading, almost pitiful.

Reluctantly I released my grip. No sooner had I done so than his fist made a cruel swing into the pit of my stomach. I didn't have any time to defend myself. Another hammer-fist hit into my jaw. I felt the world spinning around me as one more fist made contact with my body. Then something happened. Something snapped in the back of my mind. The frozen emotion so suppressed for the little bastard, who had raped and murdered my sister, suddenly sprang loose. The three painful blows had been enough to jar it free.

Somehow I side-stepped the fourth swing and returned it with one powerful slash at Eddy's face. It was one of those open-hand forward straight arm blows that can rip the nose off, if done right. Mine almost missed him. It just brushed his face. But still I felt a light giving and rush of moisture as blood flooded from his broken nose.

Backing up in agony he covered his face with both hands. "God, you didn't have to do that, mister! You didn't have to do that! Why'd you do that? Why? Why? Oh, God, I'm bleeding *hell*! Look what you done"

He was looking at his open palms. Blood covered them.

"What have you done'?" he screamed. "*What the hell have you done?*"

He looked at me with open hate. His eyes were nervously blinking. "You shouldn't have done that; really you shouldn't have!"

One red, bloody hand went into his pocket. I didn't need any second thought to realize what he was about to do. I couldn't take the chance of it being anything else but a gun he was reaching for.

I sprang forward.

My fist aimed at his nose as my other hand grabbed hold of his wrist, trying to twist it away from him.

My fist hammered again and again at his bloody, broken nose. My knuckles became red and sticky. It was some time before I realized he was limp and starting to slump to the floor. In horror, I stopped hitting him. His face was one mass of shiny red flesh and blood. Open, broken and bleeding.

For a moment I was terrified I'd killed him; then after a quick examination I stood, pocketed the gun and walked over to the phone. For the first time I realized that nobody—especially Eddy DeBray—was worth killing. Let the law take care of him.

My fingers had just touched the phone when Linda came rushing up.

"Don't do that!" she yelled excitedly, tearing the receiver from my hand.

"What's wrong with you?" At first I couldn't understand what she was trying to do. To put it bluntly, I was a little shocked by her reaction.

"You can't call the police," she announced. The sound of her voice was startlingly sharp and commanding. I think it was that demanding quality that made the strongest impression on my senses. I turned and looked directly into her face.

"So what's the new bit you have to play now?" I inquired, trying to hold back the building irritation.

"Oh, come on now, sweetie! You know you can't call the police. That will be my job—in a little while!"

For a few seconds I stood there just looking at her. The expression on her face made no impression on me at first. Then slowly my eyes began to focus on the intense, hateful look in her eyes. After that it was much like a camera focusing on a still object. Very gradually the hard, strained tightness of her facial muscles came into full view and then into sharp mental awareness.

My first reaction was that something was wrong. Exactly what, I didn't have any way of knowing. A feeling. An idea. Something was hammering at the back of my mind. For a long moment I couldn't figure it out—then it suddenly hit me—but too late!

Eddy DeBray wasn't physically, mentally or emotionally able to rape and kill all those people. One slap and he had fallen all apart. All bluff and nothing more. Was that the kind of man who could brutally beat up and then forcefully rape my sister Lynn? Who was no doubt giving it out to

143

him in any case?

I suddenly doubted it. Abruptly I began to see things a little differently. Motive was the important thing.

Then for a moment I had that sickening feeling that people get when all at once they realize they haven't been so smart after all. But that wasn't the only emotion that ripped through me. The other deep hurting was the knowledge that I was right back where I had started— no closer to the killer than before. That other thought must have been bothering me a few seconds before it came to the surface. For now it abruptly exploded like a bomb inside my skull.

Who said it had to be a man who did the killings?

The idea jolted me. It brought my eyes into sharp focus. But too late.

Linda was still standing before me. And she was holding a small snub-nosed .38—the gun pointing directly at my stomach.

"What the hell!" uttered from my surprised lips. For a second I thought perhaps I was imagining things.

"I don't think you understand the situation correctly," she smiled, her eyes squinting slightly. "I never did like you very much. You're not such a good man! Run out on Linda, would you?"

Her voice was getting higher and higher, more threatening sounding. "But now things are a little different. Like always before, little Linda finds a way to get her man—one way or another. Now this is just perfect. The police are looking for Eddy DeBray. They'll believe it when I say you caught him trying to kill me. The two of you struggled and then he killed you. Simple, isn't it?"

For a long time I couldn't find it possible to believe what I was hearing.

Linda Clifford!

There wasn't any doubt in my mind that she must be quite insane. But this was something entirely different.

Murder made to look like rape?

That seemed fantastic! Impossible!

Yet, why not? The simplest way to get the police off her trail would have been to make things look like it was a sex crime. Then nobody would be trying to find a woman.

But how long could she expect to fool the police? She had to be mentally unbalanced. How could she make it look like rape?

Yet I couldn't help feeling a strange emotion of admiration. To say the least it was quite original and good thinking on Linda's part.

"You then...?" I gulped out. It wasn't meant to be a question. Just a statement of fact.

She nodded, smiling proudly. "Pretty smart of little old Linda, wasn't it?"

"But... but *why?"* I managed, holding back the sudden mad anguish that was trying to force itself across my fogging vision. "How?"

"Oh, that's not so hard to figure out. I never liked Lynn. She was a tramp! A little trampy slut!" She shrugged her shoulders. "She was always taking my men away from me. That evening she had been shacking up with Derk—and I found out about it. So, naturally, it was a simple thing to kill her. Then Derk. Then Theresa—she's another little bitch I never liked. They learned what happened. So once I'd started killing and found it so easy—well, it wasn't so hard to figure out a way to take care of all of them. Everyone in the group that had treated me wrong one time or another. Who learned the truth. I hated them. Oh, how I hated them!"

She was screaming now. Her gun hand was lowering toward the floor and the next moment waving slightly to one side. She didn't realize that the mad fit was putting her in a very, dangerous position.

"I never knew how much fun it could be. Nobody knows the thrill of killing until they really experience it. At first I simply wanted to get Lynn out of the way. I hit her over the head with a vase. We were in my apartment and had been fighting over men. When I realized what had happened... well, I'd already choked the life out of her with my own hands I knew something had to be done. The idea of making it look like rape—it was a natural. Who would think of looking for a woman murderer if Lynn had been raped? It wasn't all that difficult. Not really. But first, I had to consider the best way to cover-up. Cutting her body like that was a brainstorm. I've worked as a nurse long enough to

145

know the best way to do that! I actually enjoyed it. Never thought that would give me such a sexual thrill. Cutting and cutting this little whore's body! Slicing off the nipples was a spark of—well, I thought that was simply *great!* Nobody would think she was beautiful ever again. Not even her dead body.

"Of course, I did all this after I'd gotten her in my car. Well, it was difficult; I'll tell you. But as a nurse, I know something about holding, lifting a body the easy way. I covered her face with a scarf, wiping away the blood so nobody could tell. Luckily I didn't see anybody. It was necessary to move her some place where she *might* have been raped. Making it *look* like rape wasn't too difficult for a nurse. I kept her body in the trunk of my car for over twenty hours until I got the stuff I needed—you know, a man's seed! All I had to do was go and get a guy—pick one up. A girl can play all kinds of kooky games. Getting his sperm wasn't all that hard—I mean, in a bottle. A new kind of game for him. Then, too, he was drugged out of his skull!

"I did the same with the other girls, too. But it was easier, this time, because I had done it once before. With Lynn I had to plan things out. After the fact. Oh, how exciting that all was. You have no idea. It was almost as thrilling as screwing you, her brother. Oh, what fun that was! With the others I simply went through the routine again. What I'd learned doing your sister in and fixing her up nice and lovely like…well, the rest was easy."

"How long can you continue killing people?" I shot back, hoping to some way talk her out of putting a bullet in my body.

"Long as necessary. The police are dumb. They'll never understand! How could they? Only men. Just men! They don't think like a smart woman. And I'm not about to let them pen me up where I can't get me a few hot lovers.

"That's the terrible thing about life. You get penned up, one way or another, but as long as they don't put bars around you—you can swing! I'd die in jail. So—what do you expect me to do? Let you live?"

All this time I had leaned forward on my feet so it would be possible to take a chance at leaping at her.

146

Linda's involvement in the conversation seemed to have captured all her attention.

I figured this was my last chance.

But when I started to move forward she suddenly, without warning, sobered. The gun leveled. Her fingers whitened as she started squeezing the trigger.

This was it.

For the first time since the war, I was facing death. But this was a thousand times more horrible because of the cold-bloodedness. Without even giving me a chance to defend myself, she was about to kill me. In the war, you had some kind of chance. Or, at best, the illusion of a chance. All of it was rationalization. When death comes, there's no escape. But until it does you fight with everything that you have to survive.

There wasn't any time to leap forward or to sidestep. All I could do was stand and wait.

Still, I couldn't just wait to be killed without doing something. Anything. My mind screamed for some way to escape death. It searched frantically. Time seemed to be standing still.

"Wait!" I shouted desperately.

She paused for a split instant. She relaxed. The only reason I can give for her reacting in the way she did is possibly the frantic sound and unexpected explosion in my words.

I was desperate, that much I'll freely admit. Never, in the past, had I thought it would be possible to beg for my life. At that moment I realized I'd do anything to get that one chance to keep from being killed. I was doing that, right now.

"Why kill me?" I questioned. "What good will that do?"

Her features frowned. She shrugged "Why not? And it is such a delicious fun game. Do you have any idea how much fun it is to simply switch off a human life? One moment they are alive, the next they are dead. Like being God! Wonderful. Just so wonderful! Better than sex! Believe it or not. Well, almost better. Maybe it is. I don't know. Don't care."

I had gained time. That's all that I wanted. Time to

have one little chance to save my life. Now it would be up to me to leap at the first instant she gave any indication that I might even have a slight chance of getting the gun away from her.

For some reason I didn't even feel hate. I couldn't feel anything toward this girl other than fear that she might kill me.

It's funny how a guy will become so selfish when it comes to his own life. The only thing that counts is his continuing to breathe. Live. Feel. Love. Enjoy the simple things. Anything.

The image of Barbara did a quick appearance before my eyes and then faded out. One thought followed: *if I got myself killed 1 would never be able to hold her form close again.*

Oddly that's what did it. That one thought. It made me realize that nobody had the right to take the life of another. When they did that they were placing themselves on a level with God. Not that I was the religious type; but I still believed in a Creator—and Linda Clifford had no right to try classing herself in such a Divine role.

Nobody had that right!

And damn it all, I thought, at the same time suddenly leaping toward Linda without warning.

Even I wasn't prepared for such action. Maybe that's what gave me the edge.

I think the attack came more as a surprise to me than to Linda. I hadn't thought about it before taking action. The abrupt change in my mental attitude had given my muscles and nerves the wild drive they needed.

I heard the gun go off. I felt burning heat ripping at my side. But I didn't stop. My arm shot outwards. Actually the next few seconds are still a blur to my memory. It seemed that the struggle lasted forever—and at the same time it was over in seconds.

The first swing of my fist caught Linda across the face. The yell of delight that sounded from her broken lips was sickening to hear. And that's what gave me my *second* edge.

Linda's almost insane pleasure in being hurt.

148

Only for a moment did she let the impulse to be beaten up and banged around interfere with her more urgent need to kill me.

But that's all I needed. That split second of indecision. It was like taking candy from a small, helpless child. Once my fingers got hold of her wrist it was only a matter of giving a gentle twist. The inner need to feel pain took over and her fingers loosened on the gun as her body relaxed and then tensed from the ecstasy of being physically hurt.

For a moment I felt tempted to yank her arm completely off. The anger and disgust at what this woman had done to so many people, and what she had just tried to do to me was damning.

Somehow I managed to restrain the impulse to beat the holy hell out of her. One reason pushed me back to reality: nobody was worth going to the chair for—or spending even one day in jail for.

She wasn't worth killing.

Another sobering thought took over: she really wasn't responsible. No woman could have done what she did and be mentally responsible for her actions. Instead of inflicting any more harm or pain on Linda, I released my grip on her arm and then pulled from my pocket the gun which I had taken from Eddy a little earlier.

A moment later I had stepped to the phone and called the police. Fifteen minutes after that the room was filled with cops and reporters and doctors. The next few hours were a hell of questions. They blurred into just one jagged series of meaningless words and responses. Flash bulbs and people pushing frantically around.

Murder Times Four, by Charles Nuetzel

☞Chapter Seventeen☜

The beach house was still one hell of a place to shack up with a broad. It was evening and the moon wasn't as bright as it had been on that other day not too long before. The sky was a little cloudy, but we really didn't notice.

The two highballs were within easy reach.

Music was playing on the record player. The two people were exactly the same.

No, not *exactly!* Things had happened to change us. But that was the way of life itself: change. The girl seemed even more beautiful than she was before. She *seemed* different. And the man, Stan Matson—yours, truly—had changed a lot. Everything was different.

The girl wasn't a "broad" any more. She'd become a very desirable woman. And I'm not just talking about sex, either! But now I could look at Barbara and see her in a completely different way. She wasn't just another quick bed-tumble. She wasn't a cheap little tramp. She was a woman worth one hell of a lot. A very classy lady.

Stroking my hair, she looked tenderly up at me.

"You realize, darling" she smiled happily, "that this is the first time we have ever had a chance to talk about...?"

"What?"

"Oh, you know. About what happened...?"

I nodded. She might think this was the time to be talking, but I didn't. Leaning down I pressed my lips to hers. The response was only a gentle peck, then she pushed me away.

"No! I'm serious. You haven't told me exactly—everything!"

"So, this is the first time we've had to relax and talk

151

about other things outside of ourselves and the future...but this isn't the time to be *talking."*

Her finger gently touched my lips, silencing them. "I want to know. It's like reading a suspense novel and then having it pulled away from you right when everything is about to be explained. I thought—"

"Okay—okay, lover. Anything for my sweet little Barbara. What do you want to know?"

"The ending. Explain. All I really know is what little I read in the papers. Linda Clifford killed Lynn Matson, Derk Meechan, Theresa DeBray and that other woman— what's her name?"

"Miss Turner."

"Well, what about the rest of the story?"

I lit two cigarettes and handed one to her. After taking a deep drag I settled down to telling her the details of how the police had booked Linda Clifford on the four counts of murder. How, later, she was placed in a mental institute for observation, and where she would probably be kept for the rest of her life. If not that one, at least one that could house such criminally insane people.

"But who was it that hit you and me in your apartment?" she questioned, brushing my lips aside away from her mouth.

"Not now," she murmured, "after the rest of the story!"

"That was Eddy. The confusing point about the whole thing was that two different lines of action were taking place. Theresa actually thought that Eddy had done the murder. She must have found out otherwise and then confronted Linda Clifford. That was the end of Theresa. Eddy thought she was the one who had killed Derk. That's why he had searched my apartment. Both of them were actually trying to help each other. Theresa and Eddy. It was a strange relationship. As it turned out, it would seem that there was some kind of real affection between the two of them."

"And what would have happened if you hadn't shown up at Linda's?"

"She, no doubt, planned on killing Eddy—saying he had tried to rape her..."

"It's a funny thing. The police had just gotten a line on the fact that the rapes were faked. It's easy to really find out. I learned that Lieutenant Johnson knew for some time before..."

"But, you mean..."

"That he just didn't have a big mouth. While I was running around chasing my tail, he hoped that the real murderer would make some mistake. This kept me out of his way actually, and at the same time directed the attention of the real killer toward me instead of the police. The only thing was, he didn't expect me to really wind up finding out the murderer before he did. He only planned on letting me keep things all stirred up. Just shows you—better not underestimate a Matson!"

She smiled and reached both of her arms up around my neck. "You know, there's one person who doesn't make the mistake of under-estimating Stanny-boy." Her voice was husky with inner desire.

"But there's something else," I told her, refusing to allow myself to lean down to kiss her.

"Can't it wait?"

"I don't think so." I watched the delicate pulse of her creamy white throat and found it hard to control the emotion in my voice. The wanting for her was building rapidly. "I found out something about myself—and you!"

"Oh?" Her eyebrows arched but she wasn't really interested.

"That I love you...

She smiled then.

"Nothing new about that. I was sure all along," she murmured, pulling hard on the back of my head, attempting to draw me toward her anxious lips. "Come on down to mother."

"You ain't my mother!"

"You better believe that!" she murmured against my cheek.

"You're more like a lover."

"Like? Only like?" she teased, pleased.

"And like a wife."

"Horrors! Surely not that!"

"Why not?"

"Well, wouldn't that ruin things for you?"

"Hell no! Make things even better!" I assured her.

"Well, we can't have that getting in the way, now can we?" Then, without so much as a pause, she added: "Oh, darling, I thought you'd never ask!"

Conversation was over.

The only thing I can say about the next few hours is: no woman ever treated me like Barbara did.

We were totally in love. That was for damn sure!

☛About the Author☚

Charles Nuetzel was born in San Francisco in 1934, and writes:

"As long as I can remember I wanted to be a writer. It was a dream I never thought would materialize. But with the help of Forrest J Ackerman, who became my agent, I managed to finally make it into print.

"I was lucky enough not only in selling my work to publishers but also ending up packaging books for some of them, and finally becoming a 'publisher' much like those who had bought my first novels. From there it as a simple leap to editing not only a sci-fi anthology, but a line of sci-fi books for Powell Sci-Fi back in the 1960s. Throughout these active professional years I had the chance to design some covers and do graphic cover layouts for pocket books & magazines."

Much of his work in covers and graphics are a result of having had a father who was a professional commercial artist, and who did a number of covers for sci-fi magazines in the 1950s and later for pocket books—even for some of Mr. Nuetzel's books.

In retirement he has become involved in swing dancing, a long time lover of Big Band jazz. But more interestingly world travels have taken him (and his wife Brigitte) across the world, to Hawaii, Caribbean, Mexico, Kenya, Egypt, Peru, having a life-long interest in ancient civilizations. His website if full of thousands of pictures taken during these trips.

www.ingramcontent.com/pod-product-compliance
Lightning Source LLC
Chambersburg PA
CBHW051923240626
47153CB00004B/1336